WHISPER OF FROST AND FLAME

COURT OF BLOOD AND BINDING BOOK 4

MAGGIE ALABASTER

Cover by Crimson Phoenix

Edited by Lily Luchesi

Proofread by Nora Hogan

1

KHALA

"We're not in the Winter Court anymore," Vayne remarked.

"No. No we're not," I agreed. The question was, where the hells were we?

We'd been in the mist, pulled there on ghostly fingers. I'd made the portal to get us out of there. To get back to the rest of the pack.

Now, we stood on the edge of a vast expanse of grassland. A breeze rippled the green-gold grass for unbroken kilometres. Behind us, a copse of trees gradually thickened into a forest that meandered up the shallow slope of a hill. A castle sat perched at the apex, squared towers made of large blocks visible above the canopy.

"Does anything look familiar?" I asked.

"You're the one who brought us here," he pointed out. "It must look familiar to you, or that wouldn't be possible. You can only make a portal to a place you've been."

I turned around in a slow circle. "If I've ever been here, I don't remember it. But..."

The commander of the Winter Court army fixed me with a look that said he knew he wasn't going like what he was about to hear. "But?"

I winced at his expression.

"In my room back at the Temple, back when I was a Silent Maiden, a triptych of paintings hung on the wall. They made this." I raised my hands and framed part of the landscape with my fingers.

"Fuck," Vayne said softly. "Once upon a time, I would have said it's a coincidence or a bunch of bullshit. But now, I've seen enough to know some past asshole put it there to bring us both here. I knew being this good-looking would go badly for me at some point."

He gave me the faintest upward jerk of the side of his mouth. More a twitch than a smile. Mostly, he glared at the landscape as though somehow it was to blame for us being here. "Did it give any indication of where 'here' is?"

I lowered my hands to my sides and thought

back to the paintings. "No. There was no writing on any of them. Not on the back of them either." I got curious one day and took them off to look. I'd asked one of the priestesses about them once, but they had no more answers than I did.

"Wild guess, the castle belongs to the Court of Dreams." He nodded toward it.

I pinched him.

"Ouch, what the fuck was that for?" He squinted at me.

He wasn't wrong about how attractive he was. Dark hair, dark eyes and a muscular body, the usually grumpy Fae was part of my pack. One of the mates I was bonded to. One of five. The other four were on the end of the bond, wondering what the hells happened to us.

"Just making sure we're not dreaming. I figured it would be more effective than pinching myself."

I jumped as he pinched my ass hard. "No, not dreaming."

"I guess that means we found the Court of Dreams." His hand lingered on my ass. "The question is, can you make us a portal back to somewhere that isn't here? Maybe after we take advantage of being alone." His dark eyes were suddenly darker.

What was it with men that we could be in the

middle of wide grassland, in the gods only knew where, and he could still think about sex? And get me going with the suggestion.

"We could—" Movement in the sky interrupted my train of thought.

A shadow soared over us, followed by an enormous, winged beast. And another. And another.

"Shit. The portal might be a good idea right now." Vayne grabbed my arm and pulled me to him, putting himself between the three griffins and me.

Before I could begin to open one, the first of the griffins landed a few metres from us. Wind from its wings ruffled my hair and clothes. I threw my hand up to protect my eyes from dust thrown up by massive taloned feet hitting the ground.

I turned as the other two landed behind, circling us in.

"When I woke up this morning, I didn't think I'd end the day as lunch for griffins," Vayne said with a grunt.

"Me either," I agreed. All thoughts of opening a portal went right out of my head, shoved out by awe for the magnificent creatures surrounding us. Along with a healthy dose of fear.

Each had a long, wicked looking beak, and round, orange eyes. The one in front of us blinked slowly, upper and lower lids closing and opening again. Golden feathers on a birdlike head led down to golden fur and haunches made for pouncing. Huge front paws were tipped with claws that looked ready to tear us to shreds.

A spicy scent, like cinnamon, accompanied each of them, a strangely pleasant balance to their fierce appearance.

Seated on the back of each griffin was a helmeted figure dressed in dark leather moulded to their bodies like a second skin. One slipped off her helmet and tucked it under her arm. Her hair was as golden as her griffin, ears delicately pointed. She regarded us with eyes the colour of Ryze's whiskey.

"You have come from the seasonal courts," she declared.

I exchanged half a glance with Vayne, trying to come to some agreement as to how we should respond.

"We have," Vayne said slowly, carefully. "Who the hells are you?"

She regarded him, barely blinking.

I couldn't tell what she was thinking. As far as we knew, these were the Fae who attacked the seasonal courts. Who killed Dalyth. Who were about to kill us.

My hands twitched. I should have asked Tavian to teach me how to use a knife the way he did.

"You'll come with us," she stated. "You may ride on the back of Patric and Gavil's griffins." She spoke like she was used to being in charge. She expected to be obeyed.

"What if we don't want to go with you?" Vayne asked. "As it happens, we were just about to get the fuck out of here. You might want to move your griffins out of the way before we open a portal in the middle of one."

She looked unimpressed, bordering on angry at his response. The griffin shifted underneath her, as though sensing her annoyance. He made no move to attack. Yet.

Another of the riders chuckled.

"They're feisty, Yala." He pulled off his helmet and grinned. "Don't worry, the griffins don't bite unless we tell them to. I'm Patric, that's Gavil."

Gavil gave us a nod, but left his helmet on. His whole body was tense. So taut it might snap at a sneeze.

I looked back to Patric. He seemed friendly at least. "Are you planning to tell them to bite?"

"That depends on you," Yala said darkly. Her

annoyance seemed to be directed at Patric. That was confirmed when she glared at him.

"I'd apologise for Yala, but she hates it when I do that," Patric said. "She'll loosen up when she gets to know you. So, who's riding with me?" He looked from me to Vayne and back again.

"We're not riding separately," Vayne growled. "If we agree to go with you, and we haven't done that yet, Khala stays with me." He tightened his grip on my arm.

"You'll hurt Gavil's feelings, right, Gavil?" Patric grinned at his companion.

Gavil responded with a very Vayne-like, eloquent grunt.

"Sounds like he doesn't give a shit to me," Vayne said. "What do you want with us anyway? Why did you try to kill us?"

While he and Yala had a glaring competition, I sniffed. I expected to find at least one alpha, or omega, but none of the riders were either of those things. All three smelled like betas. What did that mean, if anything? I sensed somehow it was significant, but right now, I couldn't see how.

"The griffins are perfectly capable of carrying you in their claws," Yala said darkly. "You might find it slightly less comfortable than riding on their backs."

"Has it occurred to you we might go willingly if you told us why?" Vayne said. "A simple explanation doesn't seem like too much to ask. Does it, Khala?" He turned his head towards me, but didn't take his eyes off Yala.

"There is a reason you've been brought here," Yala said. "It's not my duty to disclose that. I assure you, we meant you no harm. None of the incursions into the seasonal courts was intended to kill either of you. If they had, you'd be dead." She sniffed.

"What was the reason behind the incursions?" I could probably set all three griffins and their riders on fire, then get the hells out of here. Whatever their intent was, they *had* fired lightning bolts at us. They'd almost hit Vayne and me. That wasn't a friendly act, as far as I was concerned.

"As I said, I may not disclose that," she said, visibly becoming further irritated.

"You don't know, do you?" Vayne stated. His tone was derisive now, almost taunting.

"We were sent to collect you," Patric said. "Believe it or not, it's an honour to be permitted to ride on the back of a griffin."

"Says you," Vayne growled.

Patric was undeterred. "I didn't expect you to believe me. How about we show you?" He leaned over and stretched his hand out to me. "Come on, ride with me."

His grin and the slight upward movement of his eyebrows confirmed what I already guessed. He was flirting with me. He seemed like the sort who would flirt with everyone, like Ryze or Tavian. They flirted every chance they got.

"It can't hurt to give them a chance," I said. We *had* come in search of the Court of Dreams, after all. I didn't trust these three, but this might be the opportunity we needed. The chance to learn what this court's intentions were towards the Court of Shadows. Perhaps to broker peace between them. Some kind of understanding that wouldn't end in all-out war.

"It *could* hurt, but if you're going, then I'm going." Vayne looked less than pleased at the prospect. He kept his eyes on Patric while the golden-haired Fae man helped me to slide up behind him on the griffin. He glared at him, a silent warning to keep his hands to himself.

Before anyone could stop him, Vayne vaulted up behind me and gripped my waist with his wide hands.

"See, there's plenty of room on the back of this thing," Vayne grunted.

"There is, but I suggest you refrain from referring to Nami as a thing," Patric said over his shoulder. "She tends to take exception to stuff like that. It would be unfortunate if she decided to buck you off mid-fight."

"Don't threaten me," Vayne rumbled.

"I'm not threatening you, I'm telling you what might happen if Nami gets upset. Now, I suggest you wrap your arms around my waist and get as close to me as you can."

While Vayne grumbled, I shimmied forward a couple of centimetres and slipped my arms around Patric. His leather was butter soft and smelled like a combination of griffin and woodsmoke. Obscurely, it reminded me of Ryze.

I felt down the bond for him and the rest of my pack. They seemed to have left the mist and the Court of Shadows. They weren't close, so they hadn't figured out how to follow me here. If I had to guess, I'd say they were in the Winter Court, probably trying to figure out how to find us.

I sent thoughts that we were fine, and that I'd keep the bond open in case anything happened.

Vayne tightened his grip as the griffin crouched

and jumped skyward. Her massive wings snapped out as she rose, sweeping the air to push us higher.

"Fucking hells," Vayne whispered. "Don't look down, *don't look down*."

I wasn't sure if he was talking to me, himself or both of us. He put on the façade of being a big bad army commander, but in the end he was a person with fears like the rest of us. This particular one, I hadn't known about.

"Scared of heights?" I said over my shoulder, no judgement in my tone. As far as I was concerned, it was a perfectly rational fear. Especially while sitting on the back of a griffin.

"It's not the heights I'm scared of," Vayne replied. "It's the landing. Falling off this thing would suck."

"Don't fall off," Patric told us. "But don't worry. If you do, Nami will catch you."

"That's fucking great," Vayne said sarcastically. "I can't wait to dangle from those claws." He held on so tight, I could hardly breathe. In turn, I did the same to Patric.

It really *was* a long way down already, and if the griffin didn't catch us, the landing would kill us. Wind roared past, threatening to sweep us off the griffin's back.

"Isn't the view from here incredible?" Patric asked.

The other griffins flew on either side of us, a magnificent sight for sure, but a glance at the ground below took my breath away.

"This is insanity," Vayne said. "If Fae were supposed to fly, we'd have fucking wings."

Patric chuckled and leaned back against me as we soared toward the castle perched on top of the hill.

2

KHALA

The griffins landed neatly inside the castle walls. Their feet kicked up dust in a yard big enough to fit several of the beasts. The large stone structure off to one side, with huge wooden doors standing wide open, suggested they were housed here.

"Imagine having to clean out their shit," Vayne said as we landed in the centre of the yard.

"That might be why they brought us here," I said, half-joking.

"Fuck that," he growled. "If they wanted people to help them clean up after their animals, they could have brought Zared here instead."

Patric chuckled. "Don't worry, we have plenty of help to clean up after the griffins."

Indeed, the moment we stepped off her back, a group of Fae children came running to lead Nami inside the building. They must have seen her a thousand times before, but they all looked at her and the other two griffins with awe.

Patric and Yala slipped their helmets off again, but it was Gavil who caught my eye.

When he pulled his off, I saw his face was heavily scarred. Almost every centimetre of his skin was covered in what looked like burn scars.

I tried not to stare, but it was difficult. Fae tended to heal injuries with magic, if they were lucky enough to get to a healer in time. I'd never seen any with injuries like this.

He noticed me staring and turned to glare. He shot daggers at me with his eyes, before he turned and stalked away.

"What happened to him?" I asked softly.

"Fire," Patric replied with an indifferent shrug. "He was a kid at the time. He probably doesn't even remember, but he's still touchy."

"You don't have any healers?" Vayne asked.

"That's a matter for our leaders," Yala snapped. She gestured for us to step through an archway that led towards the castle.

I glanced back over my shoulder before I

followed. The children who took the griffins into their stable building came running back out and started to kick a ball around the yard. They laughed and shouted while they played, carefree and joyful.

I smiled before I turned away. "I didn't realise how few Fae children I've seen." There were none in the Court of Shadows; their High Lady forbade her people from breeding.

Here, they seemed to have space in abundance. If I had to choose between the two courts, I might be inclined to choose this one. If I trusted anyone here that wasn't me or Vayne.

"Most of them are occupied with studies or chores," Vayne said. He frowned at the playing youngsters as though they were wasting their time somehow.

"Here, we like children to be children," Patric said with a shrug.

Vayne muttered something I couldn't catch, then laced his fingers through mine and tucked me against his side. He gave Patric a look as though if he thought about touching me, Vayne might stab him through the eyeball.

Patric merely grinned in response. He seemed like the kind of man who wasn't bothered by much.

Nor was he easily intimidated, judging by his inter-actions with Yala.

We followed them through the arch and a set of worn, stone steps to a wide terrace. Yala led the way across to a set of doors which were thrown open to the afternoon sunshine.

We stepped into a room tastefully decorated with mahogany furniture and pale, timber floors. Every-thing in the room was simple, and placed with care. Couches and armchairs sat within reach of several tables, and footstools upholstered in dark fabric. If the room was occupied with people, no one would sit with their back to anyone else. Nor would anyone sit with their back to the doors.

The space was comfortable, cosy. The perfect room to sit and read a book, or share too much wine with friends.

Yala took us all the way through that room and out the door on the other side.

We stepped into a darker, more utilitarian corri-dor. No art occupied any part of the walls. The windows we walked past were narrow slits, as though for defence against invaders.

"This is an older part of the castle," Patric explained. "It dates back over a thousand years. The terrace and sitting room are only about five hundred years old."

"Only," I echoed. Sometimes I forgot how old Fae got. Five hundred years was young for a lot of them.

Patric chuckled. "I was a child when it was built. Before that, the front of the castle was a crumbling ruin."

"This way," Yala snapped, as if we weren't keeping up with her steps. Perhaps she was irritated with our small talk. As far as I could tell, she was easily irritated.

She led us down the corridor, into a large reception room. This one looked like a combination of the old castle and the new. The windows were slits, but the room was full of the same style of furniture as the sitting room. Simple, hand carved and comfortable. Each of the chairs was padded and upholstered in similar dark fabric.

Several Fae looked up as we entered the room, all of them with hair in varying shades of gold. None was more than a shade or two darker, or lighter than the griffins's fur.

Back when I was still a Silent Maiden, I saw pictures of lions in the Temple library. Creatures that looked like the back half of a griffin, but with heads like cats, with heavy manes around their faces. I was reminded of those now. These Fae looked like a pack of lions and lionesses.

"High Lord Dennin, High Lady Ramela," Yala greeted two of them. "I have brought the outsiders. They come with many questions."

She said that as though having questions was a bad thing. Like we were children who needed to know the answers to anything and everything.

"Thank you, Yala." Ramela rose from her chair, took Yala's hands in hers and pressed her forehead lightly to the other woman's. She released Yala's hands and did the same with Patric.

Vayne's hand tightened on mine, not with possessiveness this time, but hoping she wasn't expecting him to do the same thing with her.

I remembered what he told me about an older Fae woman taking advantage of him when he was a much younger man. He was grumpy with everyone, but particularly women who weren't me. When we met, I thought he hated me. Now I knew it was only his past talking. Nothing I could blame him for, especially given what Wornar did to me. Thanks to Cavan, that was now a slight pinch in the back of my mind, not the heart-shattering event it was at the time.

Ramela cast a glance at us, but didn't offer either

of us her hands. Presumably the greeting was reserved for members of her court, or her friends. Instead, she waved us over to chairs.

"Please, sit. Patric, darling, go and organise us some refreshment." She waved him away like he was still a child.

Far from looking offended, he grinned and nodded before he backed out the door.

"I'd imagine you have a great many questions," Dennin started. "So do we."

Ramela gave him a glance. "Let's start with their names."

Vayne introduced us and then said, "You have a High Lord and a High Lady? Which one of you is really in charge?"

Dennin offered Ramela a sly smile. "In theory, we're equals, but anyone who knows us, knows I often defer to my very wise wife."

The look she gave him back was openly adoring. "And he calls me the wise one. A wise man knows when to listen to a woman, wouldn't you agree, Khala?"

I couldn't help but smile. "That sounds accurate to me. More men should listen to what women say."

"I always listen to what you say," Vayne argued. "So do the rest of the pack."

"Pack?" Ramela asked. "Are you not husband and wife?"

Vayne grunted. "Not yet."

That was the first time any of my men mentioned marriage. I hadn't even thought about it before. Could I marry all of them? I liked the idea, but would they? That was a thought for another time and definitely another place.

"I have five mates," I said finally. I realised, to my surprise, no one else in the room was an omega or an alpha. I hadn't smelled the scent of either since arriving here. What did that mean, if anything?

"All male," I added.

"Five men," Ramela mused. She looked at Dennin sideways.

He snorted. "Don't even think about it. I'm not sharing you with four other men."

She sniffed, but smiled. "We might have to talk about that later."

"Only if you want me to start having to kill anyone you take an interest in," Dennin said. "I could start with Patric."

Ramela laughed. "Breia forbid. He's too young and frivolous for me."

"You worship Breia?" I asked without thinking. The temple that housed the Silent Maidens was dedicated to the goddess Breia. I hadn't known any of the Fae believed in her, much less worshipped her. Granted, I hadn't had much in the way of theological conversations with any of the Fae, beyond Cavan's apparent disbelief the gods existed at all.

Ramela cocked her head at me. "Of course. She is our goddess. The goddess. Mother of all existence."

The Temple didn't mention her as more than one of the minor gods, in spite of having her own temple. She certainly wasn't considered the mother of anything other than a couple of younger gods.

Beliefs certainly had changed in the last thousand years.

"You were a Silent Maiden, were you not?" Ramela straightened her head and raised eyebrows in question. Her expression remained pleasant, but with an air of urgency. Of the need to know. Whatever was going on here, a lot was at stake for them.

Me too, I thought. I hoped I was whatever she needed me to be, because I didn't know what would happen if I wasn't.

I wasn't sure how much I should tell them, but I nodded. "I used to be, yes," I signed. If the Court Shadows still understood maidens' hand language, then logically the Court of Dreams would as well.

Both Ramela and Dennin followed my symbols

and nodded. Clearly they both knew what I was saying. Or at least, enough to get the idea.

"I see you're wondering what that has to do with you and the Silent Maidens," Ramela said. "It was us, the Court of Dreams, who founded the order. Based on a vision from one of our own that one day the Silent Maidens would be our undoing and our salvation."

For the first time, she looked uncomfortable. I wanted to ask what her perception of the Court Of Shadows was. That the two courts were very different was obvious. Apart from Yala, everyone here seemed friendly, almost warm. They were a stark contrast from Lyra and Vernissa, and the division inside the Court of Shadows.

I sensed we would get to that subject when they were ready to steer it that way. So far, I saw no sign of animosity. No hint that these Fae drove the other court literally underground.

What was it Ryze said? When there were two opposing views, the truth was often somewhere in the middle. I suspected that might be the case here. Either way, they seemed more receptive to peace than I'd anticipated. That immediately put me on guard.

It was Zared who said if anyone seemed that

nice, those were the ones you shouldn't trust. No one was ever *that* nice.

I could have used him and the rest of my pack with me right now. What would they have made of this place?

Dennin sat forward in his chair and placed his hands on his knees. "Undoing and salvation. The question is, which of them are you?"

3

VAYNE

"*W*hat the hells sort of question was that?" I growled.

I looked over to Khala who was standing near the window face turned towards the late afternoon light. She was so fucking beautiful she almost made my heart stop. Even when she looked human and I was pretending to hate her, and all other humans, she was still the most beautiful woman I ever set eyes on. Gorgeous on the outside and feisty and sassy on the inside.

She saw right through my gruff façade, past my inner asshole and into the deepest parts of me. If I had to admit it, I'd say I fell in love with her the moment I saw her step out of the carriage into the rain. The way her clothes clung to her body, displaying her peaked nipples, full breasts and the curves of her hips. She transitioned to the way she looks now, but she didn't lose her curves, or a drop of her attitude. We gave each other hells and I loved every minute of it.

"One I don't have the answer to." She turned around to face me, and crossed her arms under her breasts. "I'm just me, Khala. Why should I be anyone's downfall or their salvation?"

I finished kicking off my boots and stood to take her hands. "This is going to sound corny as fuck, and if you tell any of the others I said this, I'm going to deny the hells out of it."

I took a moment before I spoke again. "You're *my* salvation. Before you, I thought I was stuck with Ryze and Tavian, spending most of my time training soldiers for a war that may never come. Following Ryze on his insane missions and quests in my spare time. Trust me when I say you haven't seen anything yet, when it comes to Ryze and his harebrained shit. Tavian too.

"But now, things make sense." I hesitated again. "All right, a lot of things still don't make sense, like how the hells you brought us here when you've never been here. But you... *You* make sense."

I put a finger to her lips when she started to speak.

"Let me finish, or I won't." When she nodded her understanding, I lowered my hand.

"I guess what I'm trying to say is, I love you. Even when I thought you were nothing but a human pain in my ass, I loved you. I thought my heart was cold and dead, but some of it is still alive. What's left is all yours."

I swiped a tear off her cheek and cursed myself. Great, now she was fucking crying because of me. I assumed I'd misjudged her feelings, but at least I told her what I was feeling. I got that off my chest and now we could get on with figuring out more important things.

I dropped her hands and started to step away.

She grabbed my arm, pulled me back and placed her hand on the back of my head. She drew me closer and pressed her lips to mine.

Gods, the taste of her mouth. She was better than wine, more intoxicating. Immediately more addictive. When she pulled her mouth away, I felt bereft. Like she took away my air.

And then she spoke.

"I love you too," she said softly.

I let out a breath I was *totally* aware I was holding. "Thank fuck for that. This could have gotten really awkward." I managed a faint smile. I didn't smile often, but for her I would try to do it more. I *wanted* to do it more. She gave me things to smile about.

She laughed, a sexy little sound from the back of her throat—one of my favourite parts of her—and kissed me again.

"Once, you said someday you might put your cock in my pussy," she said. "Why not today?"

After our meeting with the High Lord and Lady, we were shown to one of their fancy ass rooms to rest and contemplate Dennin's question. I couldn't remember the last time I was alone with her, but it seemed like a smart move to take full advantage of it. I wasn't going to make it too easy on her though.

"I don't know if your pussy is ready for my cock," I teased. "I wouldn't want to wreck her." That was a flat-out lie and we both knew it. I wanted to wreck her and then some. I wanted to fuck her so hard she couldn't walk for days. As far away from everyone else as we were, I would take full advantage of it. Every second. Every drop.

"You really think you can?" she asked, the lift of her chin matching the challenge in her eyes.

I returned her look with a mild one, then snaked

my hand around the back of her head and grabbed a fistful of hair.

"You like to live dangerously, don't you, woman?" I growled. "You know what provoking me gets you? Do you?"

She let out a tiny gasp of surprise, but leaned into my hand.

"Are you going to punish me, Commander Vayne?"

I grabbed hold of my belt buckle and worked it loose. I slid the belt free of my pants and pulled her over to the bed. It wasn't one of those nests omegas prefer. It was a regular, four poster bed with curtains of the same dark fabric they seemed obsessed with around here.

I pulled her wrists up and looped the belt around them. I pushed her until she knelt on the bed and tied the other end of the belt to the bed frame. She had to kneel all the way up, arms stretched above her head.

Her cheeks were pink with excitement.

One of the best things about the bond was knowing how much she was enjoying this already. She was so aroused, her pussy would be dripping.

I leaned in until my face was almost touching hers. "You're right, I'm going to punish you. I'm going to punish you until you learn to do what I say. Do you understand?"

When she didn't respond, I raised my eyebrows at her. "I said, do you understand?"

"Yes, sir," she replied. Practically purred the words.

"That's better." I undid the front of her pants and yanked them down her hips. I worked them off her legs and threw them over my shoulder. I hooked my fingers in the waistband of her panties and tore them off.

"Remind me to get you some leather panties, with a lock only I have the key for," I said.

They wouldn't keep any of the other men from getting to her pussy, but it would slow them down. Plus, imagining her like that made me harder than stone.

I turned her until her cute little ass was facing me. I ran my hand over the smooth, rounded surface of her skin. She was taut, but soft at the same time.

I crouched down and nipped her before giving her a gentle slap.

"Wait there for a moment." She could work her hands loose if she wanted to, but I wanted her to stay dangling where she was.

"Yes, sir," she replied.

Gods, hearing her say that made my balls heavy as fuck.

I pushed myself off the side of the bed, hurried over to her pack and pulled out her hairbrush.

I sat down beside her and ran the bristled side lightly over her ass.

"Do you want to use the same safe word you use with Cavan, or do we want one just for us?" I watched in fascination as her skin quivered in response to the brush.

"We need our own, sir," she replied. "One just for us."

I nodded slowly. "What about turnip?"

She laughed softly. "Turnip?"

"Why not turnip? It's not something most people shout out during sex. Not in my experience anyway." The gods only knew what other people did. That was their business.

"Turnip it is then," she said.

"Turnip it is then what?" I pressed the bristles against her skin.

"Turnip it is then, sir," she replied. "Are you going to punish me for that?"

"Definitely." I turned the brush and brought the hard side down on her ass.

She jumped slightly, but didn't flinch away.

Through the bond, I felt the sting of pain, but the rush of pleasure. Yes, she enjoyed that very much.

I smacked her cheek again, then gave the same treatment to the other side. Her ass was soon a lovely shade of red.

"Harder," she groaned.

"You want it harder? You don't get to decide, remember? I'm in charge here. If you want it harder, you have to beg me for it." By now, my cock was harder than my sword. And desperate to slide into her sheath.

"Please, sir." Her voice was breathless. "Please, spank me harder."

I spanked her hard enough to make myself grunt with the exertion. The impact made her cry out, but that tapered off into a moan.

"You like that?" I spanked her other cheek just as hard.

"Yes, sir." Her voice was almost a whimper. "Please, sir, I need your cock. I need you to fill me. Turnip. Turnip, please."

I tossed the hairbrush aside and reached up to release her hands. While she flopped down onto the mattress, I shed my clothes, and stroked my hand up and down my throbbing erection.

"You want this?" I raised one eyebrow at her. "You

have to touch yourself first. Touch your beautiful pussy."

She locked her eyes on me and dipped her hand down between her legs. She started to trace circles around her clit with the tips of her fingers.

"Put your fingers inside yourself," I ordered. I was turned on so hard right now. The sight of her with her fingers sliding up and down, then inside her pussy almost made me lose my load in my hand.

"Let me taste."

She slipped her fingers between my lips.

I sucked them, tasting her sweet flavour.

"Good girl, make yourself come." I sat beside her and watched her finger fuck herself, while I traced circles around her nipples with the pad of my thumb.

Her breath came in short pants. She closed her eyes.

"Open them. I want your eyes on me when you come."

Her eyelids fluttered open again. She locked her gaze on mine and moaned softly. She rocked her hips against her hand until she cried out. I watched her shatter at the same time as I felt it through the bond.

"Good girl," I said. "I think you deserve a reward

now. You deserve my cock." I gripped her legs and pulled them, and her, toward me until I could drape them over my shoulders.

I positioned my cock at her entrance and finally, finally sank inside her beautiful body.

There was nothing better in this world than being inside the woman I loved. Feeling her around my cock, enjoying the way she felt so full that it radiated through the bond.

I forced myself not to come undone too quickly. To thrust slowly and evenly into her, drawing out every moment as long as I could. I wanted to do this all day, and all night. I might have, but she came again, stealing an orgasm from me like a little thief.

I thrust inside harder and harder, faster and faster until my balls exploded my heated cum inside her delicious pussy.

I panted for a while before I lowered her legs down to the mattress. I drew her to me and kissed the top of her head.

"I trust you've learnt your lesson," I teased.

"What I've learned is that being bad is good," she replied. "I might need to keep being bad so you can punish me more later."

"Remind me to spank you harder later." I would, and I knew she'd enjoy every fucking moment of it.

4

CAVAN

I paused my pacing to regard Ryze.

The High Lord of the Winter Court looked calmer than I felt. He couldn't possibly have been. Ever since we left the Court Of Shadows, we'd gone back and forth about what to do.

All we knew was that Khala made a portal in the mist and she and Vayne stepped through it. Wherever they were, they were so far the bond was stretched almost to breaking point.

So were we.

Zared and Tavian barely said a word. Instead, Tavian played with a knife while Zared favoured Ryze and I with glares, as though somehow all of this was our fault.

"What do you mean Harel is right?" I asked Ryze.

Ryze swirled his whiskey around in his glass. "I didn't say he was right. I said he *might* be right. Or at least, Autumn Court legend might be right. They believed the now not-so-lost courts jumped on ships and sailed away."

"I hope he's wrong, because that's a lot of ocean you need to freeze to get to Khala," Tavian remarked.

I watched his mouth move as he spoke. I shouldn't be thinking about his mouth right now, I certainly shouldn't be thinking about how his lips felt wrapped around my cock. The memory made my balls heavy.

I pushed the thoughts away and shook my head. "If Khala can open a portal to wherever she is, then we should be able to do the same."

"In theory, yes," Ryze agreed. "I'm sure you've tried. I know I have."

I resumed pacing. I *had* tried. Multiple times. I even tried piggybacking on the bond, to force a portal to open where she was.

That was a tentative effort at best. I was scared of breaking the bond if I pushed my magic at it too hard. I resolved to try again later though, because her safety was more important to me than my ego. More important than the ability to feel her emotions in the back of my mind. Right now, it seemed she and Vayne were having fun. Presumably, their lives weren't in immediate danger.

I wished I'd gone through the portal with her. Not just because I'd be the one spanking her right now, but she wasn't as experienced in the creation of portals as Ryze and I were. As far as I could tell, she hadn't tried to make one back here yet.

Of course, she managed to achieve what we had been trying to do anyway. She found the Court of Dreams. When she and Vayne weren't fucking, no doubt she was talking to their High Lord and trying to broker a peace between the two formally lost courts.

I was sure I wasn't the only one hoping she wasn't adding another High Lord to her pack. We would support everything she did, but two massive egos was enough for one pack. The gods knew Tavian, Zared and Vayne had enough arrogance to spare as well.

"Did we try hard enough?" I asked rhetorically. "It might be we don't have the right kind of magic to make a portal to her current location."

"We are not asking Wornar," Zared growled.

"Or Harel." Tavian's tone matched the human's.

I had to give Zared credit for so fully shaking off the block Dalyth put in his head. I'd hated asking her to do it. Blocking people's memories, messing with their minds...

It wasn't something I relished. It was simply something I'd had to do, a decision I made sometimes in the last twenty years, because I had no choice. I knew the lost courts would return and I had to do whatever was necessary to be ready.

Humans running around Fraxius with the memories of the Summer Court, and being taken from the Temple, weren't in the best interests of that goal. From what Khala told me about her friend Tyla, the women with altered memories got on with their lives, exactly as I hoped.

When I ordered Dalyth to block Zared's memories, I firmly believed it was in his best interests. And to some extent, mine.

The moment I saw her in my reception room, I had to have her. It didn't hurt to have Zared out of the way.

When he regained his memories, I was convinced she would turn from the rest of us, back to him. But she hadn't. She chose all of us, and for that I was eternally grateful.

"No, we're not asking either of them," Ryze agreed. "There must be someone. Some way."

I rubbed the back of my neck. "I know of no one

who has the same ability Khala does. I would suggest we try Hycanthe, but no one knows where her or Jezalyn are. Or if they're still alive."

I got no impression that Khala found them in the Court of Dreams. They might still be lost in the mist.

Try as I might, I couldn't get the image of the mist curling around them out of my mind. It wound round their eyes and mouths and drew them inwards. The expressions of terror on their faces, the way they opened their mouths to scream, but no sound came out...

Those were images which would stay with me for the rest of my life.

I fought in wars. I've seen death and fear. But I've never seen misty claws gripping bodies, clenching them close, claiming them, pulling them until all signs of them were gone.

All that was left was a wall of mist, taunting me. Telling me I couldn't have them. It hadn't wanted me. It wanted the two women.

In that moment, I understood Ryze's fear of the mist. Not to mention the legend of something living under Nallis. Whatever kind of monster it was, I didn't want to see it again.

"I don't understand why she hasn't tried to come back yet," Zared said.

We all knew what he meant. He did understand, but he didn't like it. He was talking out of frustration and a growing sense of powerlessness.

We had agreed to approach the Court of Dreams on behalf of the Court of Shadows, but we hadn't agreed to this.

"We will get her back," Tavian told him. He slipped his arm around Zared and pulled him close. They were adorable together. The human man and the male Fae omega.

While I had no interest in Zared, my feelings for Tavian were complicated at best. I'd had male lovers in the past, but never as part of a pack. Certainly never one who wanted me to kiss another High Lord. The idea was...intriguing.

I wasn't sure Ryze and I didn't share too much animosity to contemplate any kind of romantic relationship between us.

I stopped pacing, leaned against the wall and crossed my arms over my chest and my legs at my ankles.

"If Ryze is right about Harel and the Autumn Court's legend, they may have some idea where the Court of Dreams went." They may have left people, or documentation, behind. As Ryze would say, an arrow to point the way would have been very helpful.

"Potentially," Ryze agreed. "Why go so far though? If they were the antagonists, the Court of Shadows were chased underground. Why leave Jorius altogether?"

"Maybe they weren't leaving Jorius," Tavian said. "Maybe they were going somewhere."

"So they weren't running," Zared said slowly. "They were deliberately going...wherever they are, for some particular reason. Griffins?"

"Potentially," Ryze agreed. "Vernissa said they tamed the griffins for the purpose of attacking the Court of Shadows."

"I saw a vision of them doing just that." Tavian shivered.

"Right," Ryze agreed. "It's possible they moved away to put a plan in motion to finish what they started."

"That is some foresight," I remarked. Most of the Fae I knew were planners, but not usually to this extent. Abandoning their lands and cities just so they could later annihilate their enemies was something very different. Whatever went on between the two courts, that was a lot of time and work to invest in a grudge.

"We've always thought they were in this for the long game," Ryze said. "Everything seems to indicate the Fae of a thousand years ago had plans that are only now coming to fruition."

"What about Illaria?" Tavian asked. "She's the heir to the Autumn Court. If anyone knows where the Court of Dreams might be, she would."

I remembered her from the dinner with Harel. She'd claimed to want to reconcile with her father, before helping Khala steal what turned out to be a fake key. Harel had switched out the real one and not told his daughter.

Wherever her loyalty lay, it wasn't with him.

"I saw her in the training yard earlier," Zared said. "She's always very friendly to me."

Tavian grinned. "I bet she is. Whenever you're around, she needs a handkerchief to wipe the drool off her chin."

He seemed unconcerned. He was the kind of man who didn't mind sharing his lovers, as long as he got his time with them too. He was easily the sweetest assassin I ever met. Most of them were quiet and kept to themselves. Occupational hazard, I presumed. But Tavian, he was nothing like that. He was deadly as hells, but he'd smile and say nice things while he cut your throat.

Zared shrugged one shoulder, unabashed. "I can't help being irresistible."

Ryze snorted. "That's my line." He favoured us all with a rakish smile.

I couldn't deny that he was attractive too, but that was something I wasn't going to dwell on right now. We'd only just learned to trust each other. Whatever else might come, would take time.

"You're both irresistible," Tavian said. He gave me a sly look. "You too."

I returned his glance with a nod. There would be time for flirting later.

"We should find Illaria and talk to her," I concluded. "It seems like Zared should be present for that conversation. She might be more receptive to opening up to him."

"I'm not going to—" he started.

"I don't mean that kind of opening up," I said quickly. I was starting to think a large percentage of our minds were occupied thinking about sex. "I simply meant she might tell you more than she would tell the rest of us. If she has a crush on you, we might as well use that to our advantage, if it means reaching Khala sooner."

"If we find out they're on some continent, on the other side of the world, what then?" Zared asked.

"We've stolen a boat before," Ryze said. "If we have to steal a ship to get to her, then that's what we'll do. Between us, Cavan and I can create enough wind to push it along faster. And if we can't, you and Tavian can row."

He spoke the word lightly, but we all knew he wasn't precisely joking. If we had to do exactly that, then we would.

"It's times like these I wish dragons were real," Ryze mused.

"Griffins are," Tavian said.

Ryze stared at him, then snapped his fingers. "Yes, they are. On this continent too."

"Please tell me you're not suggesting we ask them to fly us to wherever Khala is." Zared grimaced.

Ryze smiled.

Zared groaned. "Vayne is right, you are trying to get us all killed."

None of us doubted he would be right there with us, even if it meant soaring over vast oceans on griffin wings.

"I don't know about any of you, but this is the most interesting time I've experienced in the last three hundred years," Ryze said.

I didn't bother to argue with him. Interesting certainly was one word for it.

"Zared, let's go find Illaria," I said.

Just as I expected, Tavian and Ryze rose too. Whatever happened, we were all in this together as a pack.

Khala's pack.

*T*racking down Illaria took longer than I anticipated. Longer, I suspected, than any of us anticipated.

"She's usually hanging around near the training yard," Zared said. "I have no idea where she goes when she's not."

"Where would you go if you were the heir to the Autumn Court?" Tavian asked. "If you were working with people who also believed in the lost courts, even when the people around you didn't believe the same?" He gave me a meaningful look.

Ryze gave me the side eye, clearly expecting me to say something. To remind them I tried for years to warn them about the present situation.

"If I was her, I'd keep a low profile," I said finally. "High enough for people to find me if they wanted to follow me, but low enough to keep from becoming a target for my father's assassins." The fact she was the only heir was undoubtedly the sole reason she was still alive. Regardless of Harel's feelings towards her, he needed her until he had a replacement.

A court without an heir could be an ugly place. The preference was for an alpha who could do magic, but they were becoming fewer. Very few in the Autumn Court, by Harel's admission.

That left the succession up to anyone and everyone if Illaria was dead. Evidently the situation wasn't dire enough yet for any prospective successors to have her assassinated themselves. Or perhaps they were biding their time. Making sure the blame could be pinned on someone else.

Ryze rubbed his chin. "Where would I go if I was going to keep a low profile?"

"Do you know how to?" I asked. For once I wasn't ribbing him, not exactly. I was genuinely curious as to the answer. He'd tried to be stealthy in the Summer Court, but wasn't successful. Someone like him always stood out, regardless.

"In theory," he agreed. "Keeping a low profile is more Tavian's skill than mine."

We all turned to Tavian.

He shrugged. "I tend to keep to the shadows. And if I can't, I go somewhere everyone sticks out. Places where there are lots of people." He looked thoughtful. "There's a tavern on the corner that's always busy. Fae from all over Jorius converge there. People might not look twice at a woman with hair as bright red as hers."

"Let's try there then," Ryze said. "If we can't find her, we'll be able to find a drink."

Zared muttered something about priorities and trudged along behind us.

I couldn't argue with his sentiment. If there was anything most Fae were good at, it was being patient. Since meeting Khala, that became more difficult.

Unlike Ryze, who seemed to enjoy a life of adventure, I was impatient to put the matter of the lost courts to rest. I was ready to settle down and live my days with Khala and the rest of the pack. Admittedly, I wasn't sure what that would look like. The rest of them were settled here, in the Winter Court. At some point, I'd have to return to the Summer Court.

Thankfully, we were only a portal away. If we were all willing, and I believed we were, we'd find a way.

As Tavian said, the tavern was busy. With the curious name of the 'Dragon and Griffin', a sign hung out the front with both creatures chasing each other around in a circle.

"Are you sure dragons aren't real?" Tavian asked Ryze teasingly.

Ryze rolled his eyes. "They're as real as men with two cocks."

"I once knew a man who had two cocks," Tavian remarked. "And since I know you're all wondering, yes, they both worked. I never could decide if he was blessed or cursed. He could fuck two people at once, but two erections is a lot to handle."

"Only if you have one hand," Ryze said. "Still doesn't make dragons real."

"What do you think, Cavan?" Tavian asked. "Do you think dragons are a myth?"

"As far as I know, they are," I said slowly. "But until recently, you all thought the lost courts were a myth."

Ryze groaned playfully. "Don't encourage him. Otherwise when all of this is over, Tave will want to go searching for them."

I raised an eyebrow at Ryze. "You mean, *you'd* want to go searching for them. You'd lay the blame on Tavian, especially when you don't find any."

Zared snorted a laugh. "That sounds accurate."

Ryze turned to him. "Meaning?"

Zared stopped in the middle of the street. "Meaning Cavan is right. You're only honest when it's in your interest to be. You don't give a shit who you step on, as long as the great Ryzellius gets his way."

Ryze regarded him for a few long moments. "You've spent too much time with Vayne." He didn't deny the accusation. He turned and hurried into the tavern.

Tavian put a hand on Zared's arm. "We shouldn't be arguing with each other. We need each other right now."

Zared didn't shake off Tavian's hand. "I know, but tell me it's not true. You know what he's like."

"Ryze likes to get his way, but his heart is in the right place," Tavian said. "He cares about all of us. Whatever you think, he'd put all of us before himself. He'd also go off and hunt dragons, given half a chance. He'd be the first to admit he likes to live life to the fullest. Now, let's go in and see if we can find Illaria."

Zared nodded and the pair hurried inside. I followed a step or two behind.

The tavern was packed with Fae sitting around tables eating their lunch, or reclining against a wide, timber bar. Here, Autumn Court Fae sat with Summer Court Fae, and Winter with Spring. Most looked like they'd come here on business. They had that air about them, like they were engaged in intense negotiation. Haggling for the best deals, angling for the best goods.

Men and women moved between the tables, collecting empty plates and cups and taking them away to be washed.

There was no sign of Illaria, but Ryze nodded toward the table of Autumn Court Fae and moved to lean against the bar.

That was clearly a cue to Tavian, who slipped over to sit in a chair at the table beside them.

Deciding inconspicuousness would be the best approach, I slipped into a table in the corner. Zared sat beside me, his back to the room.

"I know this can't be easy," I started.

He crossed his arms and gave me a level gaze. "What can't be easy?" He frowned slightly.

"Any of it," I said, albeit unapologetically. "Every-thing that has happened since you and Khala left the Temple. Finding out what she is. Being a human amongst Fae."

"Having to share my woman with four other men..." He lowered his arms. "Your— what was she to you? Dalyth would have let your people kill me back at that caravan."

Before I could respond to that, he continued, "All because the other High Lords had their heads stuck up their asses so far you didn't think you had any choice but to kidnap innocent women. No offence, but the way you four Fae lead Jorius is shit. You even have a meeting place to resolve differences and you don't use it. What way is that to govern? A fucking ineffective one, that's what. I bet none of you gives a shit that innocent humans get caught up in your schemes."

I sat through his accusations until he ran out of steam and words. Then all I could do was nod.

"You're right. We're disorganised and contentious. We let ambition and suspicion get in the way of matters which should be a higher priority than they become. Two more courts into the equation and the coming centuries will be a challenge."

He flinched. A reminder that he wouldn't be here to see any of it. I was truly sorry for that. If I knew of a way to extend his life like the rest of the Fae, I would do everything in my power to see it fulfilled. For Khala, for Tavian and for him. Perhaps somewhat for myself as well.

In spite of his often abrasive attitude, I was fond

of the man. His dedication to Khala was apparent and as strong and solid as my own. I couldn't fail to admire that. Both of us would do anything for her. And *to* her.

For me, the next eighty years would pass in a blink, and then he'd be gone. However, he was here now and I would do what I could to make the most of these years.

"When this is over, we could use your assistance to mediate between us, to find a better way to govern. That should include the human kings. We've all been divided for long enough. It's past time to end the suspicion between not only the courts, but the Fae and humans as well."

In the corner of my eye, I saw Ryze sipping a glass of whiskey. He was watching Tavian, who seemed to be engaged in conversation with the Autumn Court Fae beside him.

I thought Zared might tell me to get fucked. Instead, he nodded. "I'll help in any way I can. If only to stop people like Ryze and Dalyth from using humans." He gave me a look that clearly included me in that.

I nodded to acknowledge the silent accusation. I wouldn't deny it if he ranted and raved at me, but I was relieved he didn't. That wouldn't equate to a low profile.

"Dalyth can no longer harm anyone," I pointed out. "As to your question, what did she mean to me? She was an omega who helped me to gather other omegas. She was ambitious. Probably too much so. She had little regard for humans. She was nothing to me personally. We weren't lovers."

"She wanted you to be," Zared stated.

"I believe so," I agreed. "That was never even likely. If she wasn't an omega, I would have sent her away. She was a tool. A means to an end. One of the few who could block memories. Unfortunately, I needed her."

"Past tense," he said.

"Yes, past tense," I agreed. "Although, as long as the Silent Maidens continue as they are, someone will be needed to block their memories. Otherwise we need to find a way to safely separate the omegas from the others."

He sat forward, his elbows on the table. "Since I'm helping any way I can, let me give you some advice."

I waved for him to go ahead.

"Go to the Silent Maidens and tell them the

truth," he said. "When we get Khala back, we can all go. Let the choice be theirs. You owe them that much."

"How do you think Khala would have reacted to the truth?" I asked slowly.

He glanced down at the table, and sighed out his nose. "Not very well, but she still deserved to know. She might have gone with you willingly."

"Would you?" I asked.

He looked back up. "Anywhere she goes, I'd go. If I haven't proved that by now—"

I held up a couple of fingers. "You have. I admire that very much."

He looked surprised. "You admire me?"

I chuckled. "Is that so difficult to believe?"

He shrugged one shoulder. "Maybe. I'm not a king or a High Lord. I'm not even a priest anymore."

"No," I agreed. "You're more than that. You're a member of Khala's pack. That makes you extraordinary. She has impeccable taste."

It was his turn to laugh softly. "You Fae have no modesty at all."

"That is unfortunately true," I conceded. "We are the absolute worst. Fortunately, at the same time, we're the absolute best."

Before he could respond, Tavian appeared at the table beside us.

"I know where Illaria is."

6

KHALA

*N*ot long after dawn, a man came to escort Vayne and I down to breakfast. Neither Dennin nor Ramela were present. One of the serving staff, a woman with bright blue eyes, told us they would speak with us later. She seemed disconcerted, but unwilling to offer any further answers. The sense of urgency about the place lingered, along with one of anticipation. It put me further on edge.

We were left alone after that and no one directed us anywhere in particular, so we decided to make our way back to our room. We were barely out the door of the small dining hall when I realised we were being followed. Not by guards, but by someone or something else.

"We should step apart a little bit, and see if they'll approach," Vayne whispered. His hand hovered near his hip, ready to pull a knife if necessary.

I nodded and stopped to gaze out of one of the narrower slits that passed as windows. Vayne moved away to look out another. He meandered around a corner and out of sight.

A figure shot out a doorway. I found myself pinned to the wall beside the slit. A hand went over my mouth before I could make a sound.

"Shhh, come with me." I recognised Gavil, the scarred griffin rider. He jerked his head towards the room he recently exited.

My whole body was frozen with fear, and the memory of Wornar. The way his hand felt on me. The things he'd done. I thought Cavan's alpha-order suppressed the worst of the trauma, but now it came back in force. My heart raced so hard it hurt. If not for Gavil's cold fingers tight over my lips, I would have screamed. I managed a squeak of fright.

"I'm not going to hurt you, I need to talk," Gavil urged. "Before someone comes." He sounded earnest. His brown eyes were full of sincerity.

I glanced up the corridor. Vayne would come barrelling back the moment I asked him through the bond. I asked him to wait, sensing Gavil meant me no real harm. I hoped to the gods I was right.

I nodded once.

"I'm going to take my hand off your mouth, if you promise not to scream."

I nodded again.

He lowered his hand.

"What the—"

"Not here," he said quickly. Again, he jerked his head towards the room. "You don't have to be scared of me. I know I look like a monster, but I promise I'm not one." His voice was hoarse, like he was burnt on the inside too. Something in his tone made me look at him again. Through my fear, I saw a man who was rejected by the people around him. Discarded because of his scars.

"I'll listen to you, but you need to let me move," I said.

"Oh, shit, I'm sorry." He stepped back away from me and waited for me to enter the room before he followed. His body language suggested he was sure I would flee the first chance I got. For that alone, I wouldn't.

Instead, I sent reassurance down the bond and attempted to calm my pounding heart.

"What is this about?" I asked.

He looked up and down the corridor, then closed the door behind us.

"You're an omega," he stated.

"And you're..." I stopped to inhale the scent of him. Frowned. He smelled like nothing I'd smelled before. Beta, but not. Familiar, but at the same time, unfamiliar. The closest I could come to an explanation was that he smelled like a Silent Maiden with her choker on.

"I don't understand." I shook my head. "Are you a beta? So far everyone here I got close enough to smell, is."

"That's precisely what they want you to believe," Gavil said. "Dennin and Ramela will tell you they came here to seek safety from the Court of Shadows, from the seasonal courts. The truth is, they believe alphas and omegas to be lesser than betas. They wanted to eradicate everyone who wasn't a beta. They came here because this was a place they could set up wards."

"Wards against what?" I asked.

"Wards against magic," he whispered. "Wards against those who are not beta. They killed many omegas before they found a way to suppress us."

"You're an omega?" That explained his scent. He

smelled like nutmeg and magnolias, but the way they'd smell if you were at a great distance.

He waved at his face with undisguised bitterness. "You can see what they did to omegas. I was a child. Only because my foster mother intervened that they didn't terminate me. Instead, they disfigured me and suppressed my heat."

I tried not to gape. I didn't want to stare, but the idea of anyone doing that to a child was chilling. It didn't matter who or what they were, no one deserved what he must have endured.

"I'm so sorry, that's terrible," I said, my voice rough with sympathy.

He closed his eyes for a moment. "It's the past. Now we are simply suppressed."

I had to push my emotions aside and focus on what he was saying. That was the message he was trying to get to me here. This was about more than what was done to him.

"With wards," I mused. "Like Amethyst." I'd assumed it was the stone, but maybe something was done to them. Some kind of magic. What, or how, I could only guess at. "But you can talk."

He smiled wryly. "The initial wards prevented everyone from talking, so they had to find another way. Now, they can suppress heat without suppressing their voices."

"If they could do that here, they could do that to the Silent Maidens too," I reasoned.

"If they cared to," he agreed. "I fear they prefer a more permanent approach."

"They don't want to destroy the Court of Shadows," I said slowly, horror crept up my spine. "Just the alphas and the omegas?"

"Exactly," he agreed.

"But they don't only exist in the Court of Shadows," I said.

"A thousand years ago, they mostly did. Then the Court of Shadows started to breed with humans. Then the other courts bred with their offspring. Humans reproduce so quickly and live for such a short time, there began to be more and more of them. The Court of Dreams tried to stop it from happening. In the end, they licked their wounds and came here."

"And tamed the griffins so they could ride them," I said. "But betas can't do magic, can they?"

"No, only suppressed omegas and alphas, and only above the wards." He sighed and stalked over to the other side of the room before turning and walking back.

That explained the portals in the sky and the attacks, but not why.

"I—"

I was interrupted by the door opening. Vayne looked inside. He glanced at Gavil like he better not think about touching me, then turned back to me.

"We've been *summoned* by the High Lord and Lady," he said. He looked unimpressed at his wording.

"I must go," Gavil said quickly. "I've taken too long as it is. Thank you for listening to me." He gave me a long look before he hurried out of the room.

"What—" Vayne started.

I shook my head. "I'll explain later." I had to get my head around it first. Why would anyone want to eradicate all omegas and alphas? The gods knew we had our moments, but we weren't all bad. Were we?

"You said we were summoned?"

He grumbled something under his breath. "That's right. Wouldn't want to keep them waiting."

"For someone in authority, you seem to have a problem with people in authority," I teased.

"Because I have enough authority to know most people in authority don't know what the fuck they're doing," he growled. "No offence to Ryze, or Cavan, but it's stupid to choose a High Lord because of who his father was. Or his cousin. I'm Commander of the Winter Court army because I know what the fuck I'm doing. Tavian is Master of Assassins for the same reason. No one gives a shit who our fathers were."

I nodded. "Right." Except Illaria speculated that Tavian was the son of the High Lord of the Court of Dreams. Either she was wrong or Dennin was one hells of a hypocrite. Assuming Dennin was the High Lord in question. Or it may have been his father, making Tavian his brother. Did either of them have a clue about that?

I suspected not. I hadn't had a chance to mention it to Tavian, and he hadn't said anything to me. If he didn't know, then how did Illaria? She hadn't elaborated before she'd slipped away that night. As with so many other things, she left more questions than answers.

"Did they tell us where to go?" I asked.

"Same place as yesterday." Vayne laced his fingers in mine and we walked in what I hoped was the right direction. The Fae did like palaces and castles that were like labyrinths.

"For the record, if they decide to be assholes, I'll tell them where to go. I might only be a beta, but I'm still a badass." He nodded his satisfaction with himself.

"Of course you are," I assured him. The fact he was a beta might hold him in good stead with Dennin and Ramela. If what Gavil said was true, it was better that I was here with him than any of the rest of my pack. Although, that begged the question, did the High Lord and Lady realise I was an omega?

I pulled Vayne to a stop. "Can you tell I'm an omega?"

"Beautiful, I have vivid memories of that heat," he said, looking sly.

"That's not what I meant." I frowned at him. "Can betas smell omegas and alphas?"

He gave me a funny look. "Not...distinctively. I mean, I can smell you. You always smell nice. But you don't smell omega-ish, if that's even a thing. I guess it's a thing, Ryze talks about it. Why?"

"Do I smell different at all?" I pressed.

He hesitated for a moment, then leaned in and sniffed.

"Now you mention it, you do smell slightly different. It's probably all my cum on you." He leaned back and grinned. He looked very pleased with himself.

I suspected his favourite part of the previous night was coming all over my hair. Remembering it now made me feel hot all over again. There was something about warm, sticky cum hanging in strings from my hair, and past my face.

I batted him on the arm. "I had a bath after all that."

"I know, I was in there with you." He gripped my hand again and we resumed walking. "What's with all the questions?"

"I don't know," I admitted. "I'll explain everything when we're alone."

I wasn't sure what to make of it anyway. If he couldn't smell omega on me, then all they knew about me was that I was a Silent Maiden. Any other knowledge about me might be nothing but a guess.

I had a feeling it wasn't that simple. Nothing had been yet.

"I have a feeling about this place," he said. "It looks the opposite of the Court of Shadows. No mist. No rows of skulls smiling at us. No puzzles to get in. No underground tunnels. But I feel like it's a cover for something. Like Tavian smiling before he stabs you in the throat. I wouldn't trust any of the Fae here as far as I could throw them. I know that's saying a lot, since they haven't once encased me in stone. Yet."

"I believe in your instincts," I told him. "There's definitely something off about this place." I'd thought that before I spoke to Gavil. My instincts were also telling me to be very, very careful around here.

I felt for the rest of the pack through the bond and got a sense of them being cagey, but not towards me. Whatever they were up to, I hoped they didn't get themselves into trouble. Especially since Vayne and I weren't there to bail them out. The sooner we were done here and back home, the better.

"Who was your father?" I realised I hadn't asked after he brought up the subject. "And your mother?" Hadn't he mentioned a family business making pottery vases or something?

"That's a story for another day and after a lot more alcohol," he said. "Suffice to say I'm a distant relative of Ryze. Too distant to mention, really. And nothing I'd admit to anyone else. In fact, if you tell anyone I said that, I'll strenuously deny it." His mouth turned down, but his eyes were smiling.

"I won't say a word," I said.

We stepped into the reception room together, my pulse racing.

7

KHALA

"You must have a great many questions," Ramela started.

"We presume you have a great many answers," Vayne replied. He sat against the back of the couch and crossed his legs at the knees.

Her smile held a menacing edge. Nothing I could put my finger on, or accuse her of, but it made me tense, alert.

"That depends on the questions," Dennin said. "We may not have all the answers you seek."

"Let's start with why the griffins were attacking us." Vayne's tone was blunt, bordering on rude, even for him.

Ramela raised a dainty cup to her lips and

sipped before she put it aside on the table between us.

"They weren't precisely attacks," she started.

Vayne snorted. "I beg to fucking differ. I saw that first bolt, what it did to the building in the Summer Court barracks. What the wind did in the Winter Court. The burnt meat Dalyth ended up as, although good riddance to the bitch. And this." He held up his seared sleeve. He seemed the most annoyed about that.

"Any harm caused is regrettable," Ramela said lightly. "Except to the Summer Court woman. However, let me begin at the beginning."

"What a novel idea," Vayne said sarcastically.

I put a hand on his knee. Not to stop him from expressing how he felt, but to remind him he wasn't alone. And to remind myself.

Ramela gave Vayne a look of reproach, but it was Dennin who replied.

"Some of us have the ability to foresee future events."

I nodded. I knew that about them already. His words backed up the suggestion Tavian was related to them in some way.

"Not only that," Dennin continued. "At times we can see those points... Those...crossroads, if you will.

Moments which can be altered to set events along a different path." He let the words hang in the air.

"Those attacks," Vayne stuck stubbornly to his term, "were intended to distract us and make us make different decisions?"

"Precisely," Ramela agreed. "In the first instance, we foretold a continuation of the division between the seasonal courts. Indeed, a plan was in place to assassinate a member of the Winter Court and place the blame on the Summer Court."

Vayne leaned forward. "Who?"

"It is of no consequence now," Dennin said. "That path didn't occur."

"No consequence, my ass," Vayne growled. "If someone was trying to assassinate me, Ryze or Tavian, I want to know about it."

"The details aren't always clear," Dennin said apologetically.

"What about the second instance?" I asked. At the time, Tavian and I were making copies of the maps to the lost courts. The rest of the pack was inside the Winter Court Palace, making preparations to go to Havenmoor.

"The assassin followed you to the Winter Court," Ramela explained. "We foresaw her carrying out a variation on her original plan."

"Her..." My lips dropped apart. "Dalyth? You think Dalyth was working against us?"

"It would seem so," Dennin agreed.

"Makes sense to me," Vayne said. "If Ryze and Cavan got along with each other, what influence she had with Cavan would be diminished. If we all weren't working together, we wouldn't have found our way here. Plus, if anyone was up to shit like that, it would be her. She always was a sneaky, ambitious bitch. And she had people who followed her. Assholes who liked to kill humans for sport."

I pressed my lips together. Yes, I'd seen those very Fae, saw them kill the priests.

"So you killed her," I said.

"When the opportunity arose, we took it," Dennin said. "We hoped to remove you and your sister from the situation, but we were unable to do so."

"My sister?" I echoed. "Hycanthe or Jezalyn?" What did either of them have to do with this? When the portal opened, Hycanthe's magic became stronger. She was clearly connected to this court in some way. For the first time, I couldn't bring myself to think of her in a negative light. She was just a woman trying to find her way in this world. A world that ripped both of us out of what we knew and threw us into whirlpool in the centre of a cauldron.

"We're not certain which one," Dennin said. "The visions are unclear. Merely that one is pertinent to us. Thus the last incursion. We needed you all to move away from the mist before it consumed you. Our tactics may have been slightly heavy-handed—"

Vayne snorted. "Slightly? You could have shouted out a warning."

"That wouldn't have been enough," Ramela insisted.

"It might have," I said. "But the mist took Hycanthe and Jezalyn anyway. What is it?"

Their reaction to the mention of mist was immediate and telling. Stiffened bodies, wider eyes, faster breaths; as fearful of it as Ryze always was. As the rest of us came to be when we were face-to-face with it. Especially after it took Vayne and me. What would have happened if I hadn't opened a portal to this place?

Ramela and Dennin exchanged a glance. Dannin's throat bobbed as he swallowed. He nodded for Ramela to continue.

"We believe it's a shadow of magic, if you will. Like smoke or steam. A kind of residue. More than that, we don't know.."

"What happens to the people it takes?" Vayne asked.

"We have no answer to that," Ramela admitted. "There have been no visions of either woman since our last incursion. We cannot know if they still live."

I glanced at Vayne. He sensed their presence while he was encased in stone, but he might have imagined it. There was also the possibility he was in contact with their souls on the way to the gods, or the seven hells.

I surprised myself with a flood of emotion at the idea that Hycanthe might be dead. I was genuinely sad over the possibility of Jezalyn's loss. I liked the sweet alpha woman. But Hycanthe...evidently I cared about her more than I realised. When it came down to it, she was still one of my sisters.

I could almost see Vayne wondering if Hycanthe also made a portal away from the mist. It was better he didn't ask, although it seemed unlikely anyone had the answers.

"Have you had any more visions about me?" I directed the question to Dennin. I got the impression he was the one who had the foretellings. Another potential confirmation of his relation to Tavian.

"Or me," Vayne said. He seemed mollified

knowing that if anyone was trying to assassinate him, they were already dead.

The idea Dalyth wanted to kill him made me dislike her even more than I already had. Which was saying something, because the woman had got my back up even more than Hycanthe. I'd always hold a grudge for her enjoyment at putting the block on Zared's memories.

"I have not," Dennin replied. "It would seem events have caught up to themselves, in a manner of speaking. We have changed much of the past, but now we can only alter the present by the things we say and do now."

"Which is what, exactly?" Vayne asked. "You wanted us here for a reason. What is the reason?"

"It was foretold that the return of the two courts to Jorius relied upon a Fae with the blood of our court, one with blood of the Court of Shadows and one whose blood transcends courts." Ramela picked up her tea and took another sip. "A good many have the blood of our court, of course."

I nodded. Judging by the shared hair colour, they had that in abundance.

"We believe your blood transcends the courts," Ramela said.

I knew that already. I at least had a combination

of magics. I suspected this was less about blood than it was about the type of magic wielded by the omega or alpha. The specifics weren't relevant right now.

"We hoped to draw out someone from the Court of Shadows," Dennin said. "Someone who could play their part." His mouth turned downward.

"Why do you need them?" Vayne demanded. "What are they supposed to do? You don't look stuck here to me. And the other court... They can leave any time they want to."

"In ones and twos, they can leave," Dennin agreed. "Or they could, before the mist encroached. They may not realise it yet, but it keeps them from leaving entirely. Just as the wards around our court keep us from leaving. They were never intended to be removed. It will only take a great act of magic to remove them."

Ramela shuddered at the word magic. She looked like she'd be content to use any method necessary, as long as it didn't involve magic. Why was she so scared of it?

Even as I had that thought, I had the answer. Because, at times, magic was scary as fuck. It could be used for many things, including killing.

I tried not to think too hard about the magic that

was the alpha-order. That was evil in the hands of the wrong alpha.

I wouldn't dwell on him now. The discomfort of having Gavil's body pressed against mine had faded significantly. I still felt slightly uncomfortable at the thought of it, but nowhere near as panicked.

"So you got yourself stuck here and now you want help to get out," Vayne stated.

"That is a simplified version of the situation, yes," Dennin said. "Just like the decision to live in caverns underground was made by the previous High Lady, and regretted by the present, the decision to come here has proven to be unfortunate."

"You seem to know a lot about them," Vayne remarked.

"We have our spies in the seasonal courts, just as you have them in each other's," Dennin said unapologetically. "They have had occasion to speak to those from the Court of Shadows. Their dissatisfaction with their current situation was made clear."

"Why not ask them for help?" I asked. The situation was all too similar to the hostility between Ryze and Cavan when I first met them. Fae were good at a lot of things, but their communication could definitely use some improvement. All right, that was an understatement; their communication sucked.

"Past animosity suggests they would decline," Ramela said. "In truth, we believe they are unaware of our vulnerability. They would assume if we asked for help, we were setting a trap for them."

If Gavil was to be believed, that assumption would be right.

"All they want is to live out in the sun," I said. "They wanted us to speak to you on their behalf, to work out a peaceful resolution that everyone could be happy with. I think, if you ask for help, they'll be happy to give it."

Happy might be a bit of a stretch. Unless I was mistaken, it would be someone like Lyra, whose magic would help bring down the wards. Happy was definitely not a word I would associate with the alpha woman.

Dennin glanced at Ramela. "If it's within your power to bring someone from that court here, they'd be welcome." His expression suggested they be as welcome as a pimple on his ass, but they had little choice in the matter.

"And then what?" Vayne asked. "You all live happily ever after?"

"That is our intention," Ramela said. "This land, Brentius, looks like paradise. In some ways, it is." She placed her now empty cup back on the table and sat back in her seat.

"It's better than a fucking cave," Vayne said.

"Indeed, but it's not without its limitations," Ramela said. "Including the difficulty interacting with other Fae. We haven't been part of our own people for a thousand years. It's past time to end the isolation."

Her words were punctuated by the ripple of the ground under our feet. The whole building started to shake.

8

CAVAN

"*I* thought you said you knew where she was." Ryze directed the question to Tavian.

"This is where they told me she was," Tavian argued. "They had no reason to lie to me."

"Unless they didn't want you to know where she was, or they really didn't know at all," Zared said. "They wouldn't be the first Fae to lie." His gaze slid across me and Ryze, before returning to Tavian.

I wanted to tell him the lingering animosity wouldn't help anyone, but making a comment would only perpetuate it.

"I'm usually good at telling when people lie," Tavian said. He stepped into the abandoned tannery. "It's possible this was her last known location." He glanced into a couple of empty barrels. "She's not in there at least."

"That's good to know." Ryze followed Tavian and glanced into the barrels himself. "It's possible she returned to the Autumn Court."

"Highly unlikely." I also glanced into the barrels. They contained only patches of damp right at the bottom. Nothing which might be blood or dead Fae. Rather, they smelled like nothing more innocuous than the substances used to tan leather.

Nothing in the entire tannery smelled like anything freshly dead. Although the smell was so strong, the gods only knew what it might cover.

"The last time we saw Harel, he was unhappy with her. I have no reason to believe she'd be welcome back there anytime soon." He was well aware his daughter had told us where she thought the key to Nallis was. Where he kept it before he became suspicious that she might betray him.

"That might be what they both want you to believe," Zared suggested.

I shrugged. "Potentially, but doubtful. Harel very much believed the lost courts didn't exist, and she believed they did. According to Khala, Illaria was convinced he'd have her executed if she spoke out against his beliefs again."

"I'd love to see the expression on his face when he discovers how wrong he was," Ryze said gleefully. He rubbed his hands together.

"Me too," Tavian agreed. "Almost as much as I'd like to see Wornar's face when he learns nothing he did stopped us. That would come right before I stick a knife between his ribs."

The further we moved into the tannery, the more and more apparent it was that the place was empty. That is, currently empty. Here and there were signs of recent habitation. A fire that was still slightly warm. A plate and cup drying on a table beside a barrel of water.

"If she was here, she's not here now," Ryze concluded.

Not long ago, I would have responded to that with something sarcastic, or pointed out how obvious his statement was. Now, I didn't bother to antagonise him, especially with such low-lying fruit as that.

"I don't think she's coming back," I said instead. "We haven't seen any sign of personal items. Wherever she went, she went there recently, but with no intention of returning." I expected a sarcastic comment from Ryze, but it didn't come either. Perhaps he was as weary of fighting as I was. Petty squabbles weren't worth the time. Not when Khala was the gods knew where. I'd tried several more times to make a portal to her, but with no success whatsoever. I wouldn't give up trying until she was in my arms.

"Why now?" Zared asked. When we turned to him he put out his hands. "She's been here this long, why leave just when we're looking for her? "

"Because she knew we'd come looking?" Tavian suggested.

"How?" Zared shook his head. "We didn't even know until just before we did."

"Unless she has visions," I said. "Or unless one of us is in contact with her." My gaze scanned all three of them.

They regarded me back.

"None of us is in contact with her," Ryze said. "I don't think she has visions, but she definitely has contacts. She always seems to know where we'll be, and when we'll be there."

"She said she worked with other people," Tavian said. "I put out feelers with my own contacts, but haven't been able to find out any more than that. Whoever they are, they're almost as good as me at keeping secrets."

"That's saying something," Ryze said admiringly.

"It definitely is," Tavian agreed. "In this case, it doesn't help us much. We could use one of Ryze's arrows, with implicit instructions written beside them, right now."

"The lack of giant arrow is very inconvenient," Ryze remarked.

I snorted softly, before moving away from them and taking another look around. I fervently hoped this wasn't another puzzle we had to solve. I'd had more than enough of those for one lifetime. I suspected this was simply a case of Illaria moving on, the timing coincidental.

I pressed my finger against my bottom lip. If I was the disinherited heir of a court, where would I go? An heir who knew about Havenmoor. Who knew about the lost courts. Who said she was working with others and had tried to support me when no one else would listen. I suspected she knew we went to Nallis, and she must have known we returned. People often had little better to do than gossip about the comings and goings of High Lords, especially when two were consorting with one another.

Had she concluded we'd found one of the courts? Assuming she had, what would her next move be? Would she go and speak to whomever she worked with? Would she go to Nallis herself to see if she could find what we found?

I sighed. No, she wouldn't have done either of those things.

I turned to the others. "I think I know where she went. Where would you go if you wanted to say I told you so?" Ryze and Tavian mentioned it only minutes earlier.

"I don't usually have to go very far to do that," Ryze said lightly. He smiled at Tavian.

"Funny, I was about to say the same thing," Tavian said. He returned Ryze's smile.

"You think she went to the Autumn Court?" Zared said, completely unsmiling. "Just to tell her father he was wrong?"

"I have a feeling she's there to do more than that," I admitted.

"Anarchy is contagious." Tavian seemed pleased at that.

"You think she's gone there to overthrow Harel?" Ryze asked. He rubbed his chin. "If she was going to do it, now is as good a time as any. If nothing else, it will distract him from getting in our way."

"Yes, but if she has gone there to stage a coup, we can't go there to ask where she thinks the Court of

Dreams is," I pointed out. "We're no closer to reaching Khala."

I was silent for a moment, then turned to Zared. "In theory, we can't open a portal to a place we've never been. Have you got any idea where she might have been that we don't know about?"

"I've thought a lot about it," he admitted. "I've gone over every conversation we had. I can't think of a single place except where she lived before she was a Silent Maiden. You'd probably have a better idea of that than I would."

He was right, I knew exactly where Alivia was. I kept tabs on her after I exiled her from the Summer Court.

"Not the Court of Dreams," I said. "She didn't have visions, so she didn't find her way there through those."

"This is probably a stupid question," Zared said slowly. "Is it possible to open a portal to a place I saw a picture of?" In a rush he added, "I remember feeling through the bond that the place she ended up seemed familiar somehow."

"You're right," Ryze said thoughtfully. "I got that from her too. It was familiar, but at the same time, not. Like she'd never been there, but she'd seen it. She was thinking back about... Something."

"There was a triptych of paintings on the wall in her bedroom back at the temple," Zared said. "Grassland, forest—"

"And a castle," Tavian finished for him. "She portalled to wherever that painting portrayed. That's where she is." He looked excited.

"Have you got any idea where?" I asked Zared. "Where was the place in the paintings?"

"I have no idea," he said, looking downcast. "She told me she asked the priestesses a couple of times, but none of them knew. There's no way that was there coincidentally, was there?"

"When was the last time anything coincidental happened?" Ryze asked rhetorically. "I'm starting to think there's a reason for every little thing we do, right down to what type of whiskey I prefer." He frowned as though trying to discern whether whiskey tied into everything else or not. After a couple of moments, he gave up.

"What else has happened that can't be coincidental?" Tavian asked. "Maybe we're missing something here."

I ran through everything that happened in the last few weeks specifically.

"Of every group of Silent Maidens, three transition," I said slowly. "None of them seem to have anything to do with this. They're ready to defend themselves and those around them, but I don't think they're the key. Nor are the five who don't. Perhaps that is coincidental."

"Is it a coincidence that Khala is the daughter of your former betrothed?" Ryze asked.

"I don't think it's pertinent, but it is lucky," I said. "She could have been my daughter instead." Thank the gods she wasn't. That would have been a thousand kinds of awkward. Especially having to fend off men like Ryze when they sniffed around her.

"You could have been my father instead of my daddy," Tavian joked. He wiggled his eyebrows.

I snorted softly. His words made my balls slightly heavier.

"Is it a coincidence that Zared didn't die in that caravan?" Ryze asked.

Zared looked confused. "I don't think I have anything to do with any of it. No more than anyone else. Is it a coincidence Vayne went to the Court of Dreams with her?"

I cocked my head slightly. "It can't be." I'd seen the mist curl itself around her and Vayne. We all tried to reach out to them both, but they were yanked away between one heartbeat and the next. "Why him?"

"Why not him?" Tavian asked.

"He's not an alpha, or an omega," I said. "He has no magic."

"Apart from his personality," Ryze remarked.

"Apart from that," I agreed with a slight smile. He was certainly an interesting man. Grumpy as fuck, but loyal and intelligent. If he wasn't dedicated to Ryze, I'd steal him away to command my army.

"If he has no magic, he's no threat to them," Zared pointed out. "But the mist pulled Khala out of my arms. Why not take me? I have no magic either."

"No offence, but you're a human," I said. "Believe it or not, some Fae don't much care for humans." I knew he was well aware of that fact. That was yet another thing I wanted to fix. It seemed like that list grew ever longer, even when I took points off it. For every problem we solved, two more popped up in their place.

"No shit," he muttered. "But why take anyone with her at all?"

I shook my head slowly. "I have no idea. It could be nothing more than the mist thinking they were both a tasty snack. We're assuming someone is in control of it, but I don't think that's the case. The mist is a mindless entity that likes to eat, or at least steal, Fae."

"That might mean I'm safe to go there," Zared said. "Now, who's going to open a portal to Haven-moor? It seems to me, we have a triptych to take a good, hard look at."

Before any of us could respond, a portal opened right beside us.

9

KHALA

*V*ayne threw himself over me as the ground beneath us dipped and rose.

Ramela's cup slid off the table and shattered on the floor. The glass in the windows rattled and cracked, sending shards flying.

I threw a hand over my face to protect my eyes. I tried to grab some magic to make a wall of ice, or... something. Anything to protect us. I couldn't reach a drop of it. It wasn't even out of reach. It just... Wasn't there.

Gavil said the court had suppressed magic. He was right. I couldn't access it at all.

I forced myself not to freak out, even when the shaking became worse. I was sure my bones were going to be rattled apart.

"Fucking hells," Vayne growled. He gripped my shoulders so tight it hurt, but I didn't make a sound.

Smoke filled the air, making my eyes sting and water.

"We need to get out of here," Dennin shouted.

"No shit." Vayne pulled me off the couch with him, and tucked my head down. We staggered out the door after Dennin and Ramela.

The smoke was thicker here. Thicker still further we ran.

"It's like the fucking mist," Vayne said.

I glanced up. "Are you sure it's only smoke?" I dashed tears off my face with the back of my hand.

"I wouldn't assume anything." He pulled me forward, holding me tighter as the building shook more violently. "If we die here, I love you."

"I love you too," I said back. "But we're not going to die here." I hoped.

Dennin and Ramela stopped so suddenly we almost ran into the back of them.

"We can't go this way," Dennin shouted.

The ground had cracked open in the middle of the corridor, leaving a huge gap. Too far to jump. Too far, I presumed to drop to whatever was below this level. I couldn't make out whatever that was, between the smoke and the darkness below.

We turned and hurried back the other way.

"Where's the nearest exit?" Vayne called over his shoulder.

The ground shook again and I clung to his arm. Chunks of stone from the ceiling started to break away and fall around us.

Before either of them could respond, the ceiling cracked and fell on Dennin and Ramela. At the same time, the floor beneath them gave way, taking them down with it.

I caught a glimpse of shock and fear on their faces and then they were gone.

Another gaping hole slanted across the building.

"Fuck," I muttered. I stood staring at where they were just standing. I blinked, unable to believe what I saw. They were right there and then...

"I wish," Vayne replied. "Fucking would be better than this bullshit. Come on, we'll need to find our own way out."

The gap behind us was widening, the floor falling away as though chasing us.

Now would be a really good time to be able to use magic, but there was still nothing there. I was going to be pissed off if I died here because of that.

"I think we came in this way." I pointed down a side corridor.

"They all look the same to me, but it's as good a direction as any."

We staggered down past the narrow window slits, all but feeling our way by the time we got to a wide entrance hall.

The smoke was so thick, I felt like it was coating my lungs, making it hard to breathe. We both started coughing.

"I think I found a door— Fuck." Vayne grunted.

"What?" I asked.

"It's locked. We're going to have to kick the fucking thing down. Stand back a bit."

I took a step or two away.

He raised his booted foot and slammed it hard against the lock. The door didn't budge. He kicked again and again, until it finally began to give way.

"Just one more—" He kicked and the door flew open. He flew through it and disappeared.

The entryway was flooded with light, but the smoke was thicker than ever.

"Vayne?" I called out. My hands in front of me, I felt for the doorway. I found the door frame and moved slowly past it and outside.

"Vayne?" I called out again. The only response was shouting coming from other parts of the castle. All muffled by the smoke.

I shouted his name out several more times, but the smoke kept throwing my voice back at me.

I walked carefully, looking for holes in the ground he might have fallen into. I felt for him through the bond. He was there on the other end, but I couldn't tell where. I wasn't even sure if he was hurt or lost. He was just...alive somewhere, somehow.

I kept moving, hoping the smoke would thin as I made my way away from the building. And hoping like hells I didn't fall down the hill. Was that what happened to Vayne? I didn't think so. He had to be here somewhere.

Every so often, I called out his name. If it wasn't for the bond, I'd assume he met the same fate as Dennin and Ramela. I presumed they were both dead. If the ceiling falling didn't kill them, the drop would have. What would that mean for the Court of Dreams? I could only guess at how many people agreed with Gavil. Was it possible they were behind whatever was going on?

As if to punctuate my thoughts, the ground shook again. I put my arms out to either side to keep from falling, fingers splayed. Someone not far from me screamed. Female, by the sound of it.

I turned towards the sound and stepped carefully.

"Hello? Is anyone there?" I called out tentatively. As soon as I did, I wished I hadn't. If this was some kind of attack, it might be better if the attackers didn't know where I was. They might mistake me for an enemy. Hells, depending on who they were, I might *be* the enemy.

I tripped over something and almost fell to my knees. I caught myself at the last moment and glanced down.

A woman lay on the ground, eyes open and staring, golden hair fanned around her head. I couldn't see what killed her, but she was definitely dead.

Was she the one who screamed?

I crouched down and brushed hair off her cheek. She was still warm. She must have died only minutes earlier. I gently closed her eyes.

"I'm sorry I couldn't do anything for you," I whispered. What could I have done? I had no idea, it seemed like the thing to say.

In case whatever killed her was still nearby, I rose and hurried off through the smoke.

I tried to orient myself. I recalled seeing a road leading up the hill to the castle. If I could find that, I could get down to the forest and grassland. The smoke might not be so thick down there. Better yet, it might not be there at all.

I walked slowly, gradually heading downhill, but across at the same time. Sooner or later, I'd find the road. Unless the gods decided to fuck with me. Since they seemed to enjoy doing that, I walked more carefully, while at the same time, moving as quickly as I could.

I kept my senses open for sounds and smells, anything that would give me a clue to where I was and where to go. And where Vayne was.

The smoke didn't let up, but the smell faded. It became less acrid, but thicker. This wasn't smoke anymore. It was mist. How was it here, in this place? Was it also hungry for Fae? Had it taken Vayne?

Had it somehow followed me here? When I opened the portal, it might have found a way to slip in with Vayne and me. If that was the case, I was responsible for at least three deaths. Judging by the eerie silence, more than that.

I started to get the feeling I was alone here, in the middle of a white wall of nothing. A heavy cloud of mist.

"Well this sucks," I said out loud to myself.

"Yes, it fucking does." Vayne's voice came out of the mist right before I ran into him. "I've been looking everywhere for you." He folded his arms around me and pulled me to his chest.

I checked through the bond to make sure it really was him before pressing myself against him and inhaling his scent.

"You disappeared," I said. "I was starting to think—"

"You can't get rid of me that easily." He drew his head back and kissed me.

I kissed him back, my tongue skating across his lips. "Lucky I don't want to get rid of you." My words were muffled by his mouth. "What happened to you?"

He shrugged against me. "I kicked the fucking door in and then I couldn't find you. But I found them."

"Them?" I asked. Who...

I tilted my head to the side and looked past him. My eyes widened.

Standing behind him were Hycanthe and Jezalyn, their arms around each other.

"You're alive," I said. I untangled myself from him just enough to give each a one-armed hug. "How are you here?"

"We don't even know where here is," Jezalyn said. "One minute we were outside Nallis, the next we were bumping into Vayne. He said we're in the Court of Dreams. How is that even possible?"

"What did you do?" Hycanthe demanded. "Wherever we go, you somehow turn up and tip everything on its head."

"I'm glad to see you too," I said drolly. "Can you use magic here?"

"Of course I..." She stopped suddenly.

"It's all right if—" Jezalyn started.

Hycanthe interrupted. "No. I *can't*. Not because I'm not able to. It feels like there is none. What the hell is going on?" She sounded as frustrated and powerless as I felt. Maybe we should be used to that by now, but I, for one, wasn't. I doubted I ever would be. I knew her well enough to know she wouldn't either.

"I don't know," I said. I quickly told them what Gavil said and what I felt.

"Whenever the portal opened, your magic got stronger, so we know you have Court of Dreams blood," I added slowly.

"We need someone with Court of Shadows blood to undo the wards," Jezalyn said.

"Khala," Hycanthe said simply.

I shook my head. "My mother was from the

Summer Court, my magic was from the Winter Court, because of my heat."

"And somewhere in there, you have Court of Shadows blood," Hycanthe insisted. "According to Cavan, people thought their magic was from the gods. How else would you explain your ability to bring those fish back to life?"

My lips dropped apart. "You knew?"

"Of course I knew," she scoffed. "You didn't think I believed *I* brought them back, did you?"

I had thought that. I should have realised she wasn't fooled. She might be a burr in my ass at times, but she wasn't stupid. I wasn't convinced she was right about my heritage, but at this point, it was the only lead we had.

"So, if we have all the blood we need to, all we need to do is find the wards and we can shut them the fuck down," Vayne reasoned. "How hard can that be?"

"Without being able to see more than a metre or two in front of us, maybe very hard," Hycanthe said.

"We can do it," Jezalyn said with complete conviction.

"We might have to do it," I said. "If we don't, we can't open a portal. And if we can't do that, we're stuck here unless a griffin happens by."

We all looked skyward, but there was no sign of anything but more mist. The sun was nothing more than a ball of light in the haze.

"We better start looking," Vayne said. He took my hand and I grabbed Jezalyn's. She laced her fingers tightly in Hycanthe's hand.

In a chain, we carefully made our way through the mist.

10

VAYNE

I've done some bullshit things in my life, but this was close to the top of the list. The rest usually involved Ryze dragging Tavian and I into some stupid adventure that somehow didn't result in us getting killed. That included trying to save the Silent Maidens from Cavan and Dalyth. I still couldn't get my head around that whole fucked up situation. Especially the part where Cavan ended up part of Khala's pack. I'd do anything for her, to make her happy, but I wouldn't rule out giving her the side eye a few more times before I accepted his role in our lives.

To my surprise, I actually missed Ryze and Tavian. Knowing Ryze, he would have found the wards by now, and Tavian would have kept us laughing the entire time. Or the other way around. I would have shared my honest opinion as we went, like I always did.

Instead, I kept a tight grip on Khala's hand, eyes scanning the ground in front of me. Every so often, I glanced back to make sure the other two women were still with us. I wasn't the biggest fan of Hycanthe, she reminded me too much of myself, but if we lost them, we'd have to backtrack and look for them. That might be an impossible task given the thick fucking mist.

It was impossible to see very far in front of us, but it would have been good for just that—fucking. If it wasn't for Hycanthe and Jezalyn, I might stop for a break and make Khala suck my cock. I can say many things about the woman, including how willing she always was and how amazing her mouth was. Thinking about her made me hard.

Maybe we could lose the other two women for a little while. Surely they wouldn't mind.

Unfortunately, I'm a realist. I didn't want to have to find them if we lost them, and I didn't want to be in this gods forsaken mist a second longer than I had to.

"What are we looking for?" Khala asked. "I'm guessing there won't be an arrow here either?"

"I'm guessing not," I agreed. "I don't know what we are looking for, but I think we'll know when we find it."

"How?" Hycanthe asked.

"I don't know that either," I said with a grunt. "You and Khala are the ones who can use magic. Why don't you tell me?"

That shut her up for a while. Me too, to be honest. Right now, the best thing we could do would be to listen and keep our eyes open. I'd spent most of my life as a soldier, but my tracking skills were as good as anyone's.

Those skills were what made me stop so quickly I didn't know I was going to until I did.

I pulled Khala around back behind me and gestured with my spare hand for everyone to be quiet. We all fell still as statues, unfortunately reminding me of being stuck in that stone in the Court Of Shadows.

I managed to contain a shiver at that crappy memory. That sucked harder than most things I'd done in the last two hundred or so years. Especially that fucking itch.

Something crunched in front of us. Crunched

again. Slow, deliberate footsteps. Moving carefully but not concerned if anyone heard. Nothing says suspicious like someone who doesn't care if we knew they're there.

I swapped Khala's hand over to my other, and slowly slid my knife out of its sheath. I scanned the mist for any sign of movement. Anything that might give away whoever was there.

I caught a glimpse, a flash of something. There was definitely someone there.

I moved forward slowly, silently. Watching for further movement.

There it was again. A hint of dark fabric, maybe a hand.

My knife in front of me, I stepped forward again. Tentatively I called out. "Who's there?"

A second later, a face appeared, followed by a body.

"What the—" I lowered my knife.

"Rijal." Khala spoke his name as she exhaled. "What are you doing here?"

That was a good question. If he was here, did that mean the rest of the pack was too? No, if they were, Khala would have told me.

He was about to speak out loud, until he saw her. For whatever reason, he wasn't allowed to talk out loud in front of an omega. I presumed that meant he couldn't talk in front of two of them. Not that any of us would tell on him, but whatever. If that was the Court of Shadows custom, then who was I to question it, even if I thought it was strange.

He started signing in Silent Maiden hand language instead.

Khala interpreted.

"After we were taken by the mist, the others went back to the Winter Court. Ryze made a portal."

Rijal didn't look happy as he explained that bit.

I understood that. Portals were disconcerting, to say the least. Useful, but not my favourite mode of transport. I preferred my own two feet, or a horse. Still, if I had to choose between a portal and the back of a griffin, I'd choose a portal all day, every day.

"Vernissa sent Rijal back to the mist to look for us. He told them what happened with Willum and Jistun. He brought great shame on himself. The High Lady was disappointed at his actions."

"So she sent her own son away because he made a mistake," I concluded. All right, he and his co-conspirators pulled knives on us, but they only did it because they were scared to leave the caverns. Sending him out into the shitty mist was a fucked up thing to do, if you asked me.

It was probably better I wasn't High Lord, because I never wanted to make decisions like that. I preferred to punish my men and women by making them clean toilets and other, similar nasty things. Not potentially sending them to a pointless death. Ironic, given that's what war usually resulted in. Of course, it was my job to make sure those deaths weren't pointless or numerous.

"He says he earned his punishment," Khala translated. "Shame seems to be a big part of their court. Anyway, then he ended up here. He was trying to draw the mist's attention so it could end his shame."

"He was stomping around so he could get killed?" Hycanthe asked, disbelieving.

Khala glanced at her. "He considers it appropriate punishment for his rebellion. Fortunately, he found us instead. He can redeem himself by helping us find the wards."

Rijal perked up at her words. He signed something quickly.

"He says he doesn't know if that will be his redemption, but he's willing to help us and start working towards it." She hesitated for a moment. "He also says I own him now."

I snorted a laugh. "He can come with us, but we

don't do owning people around here. Not like that anyway." I gave Khala a grin.

"That's great," Jezalyn said. "I'm glad we found each other. We could have been wondering about for days."

"We still might be," Hycanthe said, but in a gentler tone than she used for the rest of us.

"We won't be," I said firmly. "If we keep heading in a straight line, sooner or later we'll find the wards, or the edge of the bubble."

Rijal signed something else, his hand gestures moving quickly, excitedly.

"If she owns you, can she command you to talk out loud?" I grumbled.

He looked horrified and hastily shook his head. Instead, he went on signing.

"He said he walked until he couldn't walk anymore," Khala said. To Rijal she asked, "What do you mean by that?"

He frowned and signed again.

"He doesn't know. He tried to keep walking but the mist wouldn't let him. I don't think it was the mist. Rijal, which way was it?"

Rijal signed again. His hands moved so quickly, at times they were a blur. Strange how different the symbols were to those used by Fae who couldn't hear, such as my sister. If they used a universal language, I could have followed better. Since they didn't, all I could do was listen.

"He doesn't know, but it was close," she said. "He came from this direction, so with any luck, that's where it is."

"Because no one has ever been led astray by luck before," Hycanthe said.

Khala looked ready to snap at Hycanthe.

I could just imagine what she was going to say. Something along the lines of, "Do you have a better idea?"

Since Hycanthe clearly didn't, there was no point having that argument. I had to commend Khala for her restraint.

And since I was the commander here, I took command. "We're going this way." I indicated the way Khala had.

Jezalyn took Rijal's hand in her spare one and we went on walking through the relentless fucking mist.

Not being able to see very far was starting to get on my last nerve. I'm the first to admit I'm not the soul of patience, but this was getting ridiculous. Although, I admit to being relieved the rest of the pack made their way home safely. I never would have heard the end of it if Ryze didn't. Not that he ever listened to my advice if I tried to keep him safe. He was a stubborn asshole. A bit like me at times.

While we walked, Khala spoke to Rijal. "What do you know of the mist?"

He signed back awkwardly while clinging to Jezalyn's hand. Again, Khala interpreted.

"He says it's punishment from the gods."

"What for?" I asked over my shoulder.

"He doesn't know. He said the mist swallows his people if too many go out at once. The gods must want the court to stay in the caverns."

"That was what Dennin and Ramela said," I remarked. "That the mist wouldn't let them leave. It seems to me like a harmless annoyance right now. Maybe people left the caverns and decided not to go back." I wouldn't have, if I got away from that shithole.

"They would bring great shame on themselves if they abandoned their court," Khala said.

"I'm sure that's what Vernissa wanted them to think," I said. Call me cynical, but she seemed to like being in control over her people. Not in the same way Ryze or Cavan were. Not even the same as Harel was or Thiron had been.

Instilling superstitious ideas into people's heads was worse than just being an asshole. Making people scared of gods and monsters was repre-hensible.

On the other hand, if they were to be believed, people leaving the Court of Shadows would have fallen victim to the Court of Dreams. In the end, maybe all she was doing was what she had to do to keep her people safe. Or maybe she believed her own bullshit.

If I hadn't been dragged through the mist myself, I would have thought she was completely full of it. As it was, I figured there had to be a better explana-tion for it than simply punishment for leaving. It was more likely to be some fucked up kind of magic. Magic had a way of messing with things when it shouldn't.

We kept walking carefully for what felt like an hour, maybe more. I gradually became aware of a strange shift in the air. Something I couldn't put my finger on at first. Everything looked the same. It smelled the same. I took a moment to listen and couldn't detect any new sounds. And yet, something was different.

"You feel that too," Khala stated.

"I'm no expert, but it feels like a fuck ton of magic," I said. Only magic had that way of making my skin crawl. It made me want to climb inside myself and never come out.

"I'm guessing we found the edge of the bubble," she said.

Half a second later, the world exploded in a blast of pure agony.

11

KHALA

*V*ayne's hand was ripped out of mine. He was picked up off his feet and thrown through the air. He disappeared into the mist, before landing heavily with a crunch.

"Vayne!"

All but dragging the others, I raced through the thickened air and dropped to my knees beside him. His arm and leg were twisted, bone gaping out of his thigh. His head lay at an odd angle, as though his neck was snapped. His skin was paler than usual. Breathing more shallow.

He was alive, but barely.

"We need to get that ward down, now," I snapped. The only thing that was going to stop me from losing him was magic. If we didn't get the ward down in time...

"Jezalyn, Rijal, stay with him." I glanced up at them both, silently beseeching them to take care of him.

Jezalyn knelt down beside me. She looked me straight in the eyes with a steady gaze.

"We'll look after him," she promised. "You two go and do what you need to do. We'll all be right here."

Her alpha scent was suppressed, but it was enough to soothe me. That and her words.

For once, Hycanthe didn't bristle as Jezalyn gave me attention. Not even when Jezalyn leaned over and gave me a quick hug. She even let me take her hand and lead her back to the edge of the bubble.

"Who's to say it won't throw us too?" She sounded scared.

"It might," I agreed. "I have to take the risk. I can't let him die." I wiped a tear off my cheek. "If we don't do this, I don't think any of us will get out of here alive."

I thought she might argue, but she nodded. "If it was Jezalyn, I'd risk everything too."

I managed a faint, forced smile. "I know you would. Love has a way of making us do things we otherwise wouldn't do."

Like bonding five, incredible men. I'd only told two of them I loved them. When we got out of here, I was going to tell the other three. I wasn't sure when I'd fallen in love with Ryze, Tavian or Cavan, but I had. A long time ago, if I was honest with myself. That was yet another reason to succeed now.

"Just in case we don't make it through this, I'm sorry for being a bitch," she said. "I was envious of your confidence, and the way people are drawn to you. I always wanted to be more like you."

I didn't think anything could surprise me at this point, but her words did.

"I'm nothing special," I said with a shrug. "I could have tried harder to be nice to you too."

She smiled wryly. "I'm sure you could, but I didn't make it easy. Now, are we going to bring down these wards or not?"

"Let's do it." I gripped her hand.

We stepped forward, our palms outstretched, both trembling with anticipation and fear. The magic could embrace us, or it could kill us.

"I feel like it's right in front of me," she said. "I don't know, but I feel like we need to touch it at the same time."

"And just like that, we're back to the puzzles," I said with a sigh. "It has been a theme up until now, so we might as well try." I could feel it too, on the edge of my skin.

"On three?" she asked.

I nodded. "On three."

We spoke together, in unison.

"One."

"Two."

"Three."

When our palms pressed the magic, sparks lit up around our hands.

"We're not dead," she remarked.

"That's a fucking bonus," I replied. Magic rushed into me like a flood.

"Do you feel that?" I said, in awe.

"It feels like it knows me," she said in the same tone. "Like it's recognising me."

"Exactly," I agreed. "The question is, will it obey?"

"Let's not give it a choice," she said.

I glanced over as she closed her eyes. An expression of pure concentration came over her face. I'd never seen her like this. If this didn't bond two people, nothing would.

I turned my attention back to the magic and closed my eyes.

Images tumbled through my mind. Memories, visions, pasts and possible futures. Most of it was a blur, but now and then I saw faces. No one I recognised, although one or two looked familiar. A woman with my hair and Ryze's eyes. A young man who looked strikingly like both Hycanthe and Jezalyn. Another who looked like Gavil, but without the scars. A woman who looked to be about thousand years old. Another young, a baby in her arms.

I realised this was the magic of the Court of Dreams. All the foresight, tangled in a web of thought. Past, present and future blended into one.

At the edge of my mind was a tug of a different kind of magic. Lightning bolts and whirlwinds. Beginning lives and ending them.

Court of Shadows magic.

Here and there were hints of heat and cold, frost and flame. Buds and leaves that turned when the weather changed.

And something else. Something I couldn't quite put my finger on. Something I'd have to think about later.

The magic called to me and I bent it to my will. Bit by bit, I tore down the bubble, dismantled the wards, shattered the gilded cage around the Court of Dreams until nothing was left but a tiny spark of magic.

Then it was gone too.

The mist around us didn't disappear immediately, but rather slowly, gradually floated away. Patches lingered here or there, but mostly the air cleared in a matter of minutes.

I lowered my hand and exhaled.

"That was incredible," Hycanthe said. She actually pulled me in for a hug. "All that magic. I can feel it all now. I'm not blocked off from it anymore. And I can heal Vayne."

"Do it," I said, choked with emotion. "Please."

I followed her back to him at a trot, clinging to the bond like it was a lifeline.

"You did it," Jezalyn said. "Good girls. I'm so proud of you both."

Her words warmed my omega heart. I smiled, then dropped to my knees beside her.

Carefully, I took Vayne's hand in mine. "He's so faint," I said softly. His presence through the bond was little more than a whisper. A faint hint of the vibrant, grumpy Fae. If I lost him now...

"I've got him," Hycanthe assured me. "You've got him too. Whatever you did to those fish, you can do that if you need to."

She was right, but I didn't want to bring Vayne back from the dead. I wanted him to stay alive.

I reached for magic. Finding it was more difficult

now, but not impossible. Some Court of Shadows magic lingered. Everything else felt distant, like magic from the other courts was more closely connected to Jorius than it was to heat or cold. That was something else to think about later too.

I squeezed Vayne's hand and pushed the magic into him, keeping him alive and calm while Hycanthe healed his bones, one by one. She started with his snapped neck, her face scrunched up in concentration.

He groaned, his face twitching with the pain.

Jezalyn and Rijal knelt on either side of him, holding him carefully to keep him from throwing Hycanthe or me off.

I felt his agony through the bond. He was even weaker now. The thread that connected him to life was thin. Painfully so. It was stretched so thin I was certain it was about to snap.

"Stay with me," I urged. "If you die, I'm going to be really, really pissed off. So is the rest of the pack. I'm sure Tavian could find a way to stab you in the ass, even if you're dead. If anyone can, he can. And Ryze... Imagine all the things he'll get up to if you're not around to keep him from doing anything too stupid."

I wiped tears off my cheek with my sleeve.

"And Zared. You know he's fit in really well with the army." I didn't know that at all, but it seemed like the right thing to say. "If you're not careful, Ryze will make him command of his army. A human, imagine that."

I was getting through to Vayne. I could tell by the sudden burst of outrage through the bond. Zared would take his job over his dead body, literally.

I pushed on. "That whole spanking me with a hairbrush thing, I really enjoyed that. I was thinking that could be just for us, but now I think about it a bit more, that would be something Cavan would enjoy too."

Vayne groaned. Or was it a growl?

He felt stronger now. He was fighting back with every drop of cranky, stubborn, Fae male arrogance he had. Considering this was Vayne, that was a decent amount.

"Hold him still, so I can fix his arm and leg," Hycanthe ordered.

We all held him while I continued.

"If you want that to be our thing, maybe we can experiment with other things. Some of the priests in the temple liked to play a game with a small ball and a paddle. They hit the ball over a table, but the paddles look like fun. Maybe we could—"

Vayne's eyes popped open and his back arched. He let out a long, low cry of pure agony. His eyes were wide, skin covered with a sheen of sweat.

We held him harder until his body flopped down onto the ground. He lay there panting.

"Fucking mother of a fucking griffin fucking fuck," he said, his voice hoarse. "That hurt like a bitch. And no one paddles your ass but me," he added.

I snorted in relief and flopped down over him.

"Thank the gods." The bond felt stronger now, clear and solid. He wasn't going anywhere. After all this, he'd be lucky if I let him out of my sight. No doubt that would make him even grumpier than usual. I was all right with that, as long as he was alive.

"Thank the *omegas*," Jezalyn said. She sat back and pulled Hycanthe into her arms. They both looked exhausted. Hycanthe in particular.

I saw something on her face I'd never seen before. Contentment. Satisfaction. The realisation of who and what she was. She finally fit into her own skin.

I was happy for her. Everyone should feel like that.

Rijal looked at both of us with awe. I had a

feeling what he just witnessed made him think omegas were even more special than he believed.

I pressed my cheek against Vayne's chest and rested for a while.

I didn't want to be idolised, or treated like I was special. I was just me. Just Khala.

Through the bond, I felt the rest of my pack asking if Vayne and I were all right. I sent reassurance back that we were fine.

"Dennin and Ramela are dead, we should go and see who is in charge now," I said.

I just finished saying that when a shadow rose above the hill where the castle used to stand. Wave after wave of griffins. Each with two or three people on their backs.

Portal after portal opened in front of them. They started flying through.

"Fuck," I said softly. They must have been waiting for the wards to be lowered so they could leave. I didn't have to think too hard to guess where they were going.

"We need to get out of here," I said.

I had a sinking feeling it was already too late.

12

KHALA

I opened a portal the moment Vayne was able to stand. I tried to visualise my bedroom at the Winter Court. So much time had passed since I was there, the memory was hazy around the edges. I forced myself to focus on what I could visualise, and the bonds waiting for us on the other side.

I supported Vayne's weight on one side, while Rijal supported him on the other.

"You two go first," I said to Hycanthe and Jezalyn. "We're right behind you."

"Hurry up," Vayne growled when they hesitated. "Let's get the fuck out of here."

Hycanthe frowned at him, but let Jezalyn take her hand and pull her through.

"Let's go home." The portal was already a drain on me. I didn't want to risk it snapping shut if we took too long going through.

"Home sounds perfect." Vayne staggered a couple of steps, but we managed to keep him upright and walking into the portal.

When we stepped out the other end of the long passage, home wasn't where we ended up.

"Khala," Ryze drawled, as though he fully expected me to appear. "There you are. Vayne, good to see you looking so well."

Vayne responded with his customary grunt, but gave Ryze an awkward hug before being pulled into a bigger one from Tavian.

"We were worried." Tavian drew me into the hug too. "Not too worried. We knew you could take care of yourselves. It seems like you found the Court Of Dreams faster than we did. Nice work."

Zared stood back until Tavian loosened his grip, then pulled me in for a firm embrace and a kiss. "Thank the gods."

Cavan waited patiently until we were done to give me his hug and kiss, his tongue sliding across my lips and into my mouth.

"What is this place?" Hycanthe asked.

"It's a tannery," Tavian told her. He briefly outlined their search for Illaria.

When he was finished, Vayne and I explained what happened to us.

"We think the griffins are on the way to attack the Court Of Shadows," I said. "We have to help them." We'd wasted enough time already.

"You need to rest," Ryze contradicted.

"We can't just—" I started.

He interrupted me. "How many griffins did you say it was? It's going to take more than nine of us against that many. We need to rouse all the alphas and omegas we can. Not to mention as many archers as we can muster. If we go after them now, we are as good as dead."

"I've almost died enough for one day," Vayne said. "Ryze is right. We can't go in half cocked."

I wanted to argue, I really did, but there was too much logic in what they said. On top of that, I was tired. I needed a couple of hours' sleep. During that time, they could gather together what and who they needed.

"A couple of hours," I agreed reluctantly. I hoped to the gods there would be something left of the Court of Shadows when we got there.

Ryze pulled me in again and kissed my forehead.

"This is one of the most difficult parts of being a High Lord. Making the tough calls."

I nodded, but that didn't settle my unease. Especially knowing how frantic Rijal must be. I glanced over to him. He looked calmer than I would have been under the circumstances.

In fact, he looked at me like he was confident I would fix this. Me and my pack.

Gods, I hoped his faith wasn't misplaced, because I wasn't so certain.

Without any argument or conversation, Ryze opened a portal to the sitting room in the Winter Court Palace. We all filed through.

"I'll make sure Khala rests," Tavian said.

"Me too," Zared agreed.

"How many orgasms is that rest going to include?" Ryze asked facetiously.

Tavian grinned. "As many as we can manage." He grabbed my hand.

"Wait," I said quickly. "There's something I need to say."

As if he knew what I was going to say, Ryze shook his head. "There will be time for that later. In the meantime, we need to rally the troops. Cavan?"

Cavan nodded. "I'll return to the Summer Court to organise my people." There was more to what he was saying, but he opened a portal and was gone before I could ask.

I sighed and gave Ryze and Vayne a quick kiss each before I let Tavian and Zared pull me away down the corridor to my bedroom.

"I never really wished I could do magic," Tavian said as he closed the door behind us. "Until today. If I could have, I would have found a way to get to you."

"How?" Zared asked. He pulled me toward the bathroom and started to help me out of my clothes while Tavian turned on the water. "Ryze and Cavan couldn't help. None of us could." His frustration was very much evident.

I understood it. None of us liked to feel power-less. This was something he couldn't kill or charm his way through. That must have chafed.

"We would have found a way," Tavian told him. "But since we didn't, we can make up for it." He grinned broadly.

Zared glanced at us both for a moment, then said, "Yes, we can." He turned off the tap and tested the water before helping me to climb in.

I sank underneath the warmth and exhaled softly. I didn't know how much I needed this until right then.

The water level rose as first Tavian and then

Zared slipped in with me. The bath was so big, the rest of the pack could have fit, but this was just right for now.

Tavian grabbed the soap and started to wash my body as Zared started on my hair.

"You know I can do all of this myself." I was fully aware that wouldn't deter them one bit. They were determined to spoil me and that's what they'd do. All I could do was lie back and enjoy it. Especially when Tavian ran soapy hands over my breasts, making my nipples harden.

In spite of my tiredness, I was immediately aroused by the touch of both men.

"Tavian." I opened one eye crack. "I love you."

"Khala, I love you too," he replied. "And I love Zared."

Both of my eyes popped open. I twisted around to watch for Zared's reaction.

He scratched his forehead, covering his face with his hand for a moment. He lowered it.

"I... I love you both too."

"That's good, since we're all naked together in the bath," Tavian said, grinning broadly. Water dripped off his chin, back into the bath.

Zared laughed softly, but didn't object or pull

away when Tavian slid up to him, sloshing water over the side.

Tavian kissed him, then kissed me. "Both of you are so perfect," he said dreamily.

"No, you," I replied, equally dreamy.

Tavian chuckled. "All right, we're all perfect." He went back to washing me, taking his time with my thighs and pussy. Even when I was clean, he went on washing every centimetre like I was a statue that had to sparkle, just for them.

Every so often, he brushed against my clit, making me shiver. I wanted more, but at the same time, I wanted to draw it out and enjoy it. These men never failed to make my body throb and ache for them. The water of the bath masked the fact I was dripping everywhere with my arousal.

Zared rinsed my hair, then started to lavish attention on my breasts. He rolled my nipples between his thumbs and forefingers, pinching lightly every so often. This wasn't about spanking and dominance. This was slow and loving. A reunion of hearts, souls and bodies.

"We missed you," Tavian whispered.

"Yes we did. I missed your breasts." Zared kneaded my breasts and palmed my nipples until they were hard as rocks and begging for more.

"I missed this beautiful pussy." Tavian slipped a couple of fingers inside me. His heel rubbed over my clit as he fucked me with his hand. Every movement was deliberate, perfectly hitting me inside and out.

Slowly, languidly, my hips rose to meet him. Delicious pressure built gradually, unhurried.

When I finally came, it was hard. I gasped out loud. Arched my back and cried as my muscles clenched around him. Water sloshed over the side of the bath and onto the floor with a splash. That, coupled with the wet sound of Tavian's hand, drove me harder still, over the edge and into the abyss.

I floated back down to earth and lay with my back against the side of the bath, catching my breath before Tavian slid his hand free.

"I bet she missed our cocks." They exchanged a glance. Something passed between them.

Without another word, they made sure I was fully rinsed, then turned to face each other. Tavian put one of his legs over Zared's, locking them together like they were scissors. Their hard cocks pressed against each other.

Holy gods.

Zared gripped my hips and moved me so I strad-dled both of them.

Carefully, slowly I worked myself down until

both of them were inside me. Every few moments, I needed to stop and stretch to fit them both inside. I didn't doubt they would, but I didn't, couldn't rush. I wanted to make this last for all of us, for as long as possible.

Finally, I lowered myself all the way down until they were both seated deep inside me.

"Oh my gods," Zared breathed. "You both feel incredible."

I felt so fucking full. I closed my eyes and savoured the feeling for a minute or two. Oh-so-slowly, I started to move. Rising and falling, rolling my hips, keeping both of them inside my pussy at the same time.

I glanced over my shoulder at Tavian, who looked blissed out. His eyes flickered open. He gave me a smile.

I smiled back and went on pumping them both while they thrust up into me. Knowing their cocks touched drove me wild. I loved that they cared about each other, and were as into each other as much as they were into me. My heart was as full as my pussy. More so.

I rode them both slowly and deliberately until I couldn't stop myself from coming again.

My whole body was on fire with the delicious,

beautiful orgasm that flooded my vision and made my heart thunder through my body. Every drop of blood boiled hot in the most incredible way.

They both came a moment after, spilling their cum into me and around each other. The sounds of both men panting and groaning in unison was the most beautiful music.

"Gods, you two are both so..." Tavian groaned. "I love you so... Gods, yes, yes, fuck."

Zared moaned his agreement, milking his orgasm for every drop before he sagged, panting against the side of the bath.

Tavian flopped back a moment later, his handsome face turned toward the ceiling. "So fucking perfect."

I panted for a while, still straddling them until I caught my breath. By now, the water was getting cold and weariness was settling in deep.

Reluctantly, I climbed off them and out of the bath. I grabbed my towel and dried myself quickly. They dried themselves and followed me over to my nest.

Lying down naked amongst the cushions gave me a last burst of energy. I might as well put it to good use.

I smiled at them both, then kissed my way down Zared's body. I gripped his cock and ran my fingers up and down slowly, deliberately, until he was hard again.

"Khala..." he breathed.

"Shhh." I fastened my lips around him and started to suck.

He dropped his head back and exhaled out his nose, apparently done arguing before he really began.

Tavian ran his fingers down my back and over my ass. He squeezed the flesh gently before kissing and nibbling his way down my ass, to the top of my legs. He spread my thighs and lowered his face between them to bite, lick and tease my clit.

I cupped Zared's balls and massaged them gently while I sucked. His hips rose and fell to meet me, pressing him deeper down my throat with each thrust.

"That feels so good," he said breathlessly.

I murmured my agreement. He tasted good, and Tavian's tongue on my clit was perfection. He worked me firmly, relentless until I came against his mouth.

I took mine from Zared's cock so I could breathe through my orgasm. Tavian didn't stop licking for a moment, not until I was well and truly back down and the stars in my vision faded.

I drew Tavian up until I was lying between both of them. I shifted my upper body and fastened my lips over Tavian's cock while running my hand up and down Zared's length. I sucked, licked and worked until they were both gasping, hard and lingering on the very edge.

I slowed in pumping Zared until Tavian came, groaning and squirting his salty cum deep into my mouth.

Instead of swallowing, I slipped my mouth off him, held his cum in my mouth and shimmied up to kiss Zared. I let Tavian's cum trickle from my mouth into his.

Zared looked surprised, but even more aroused.

I wriggled back down and wrapped my lips around his cock once more. He thrust once, twice before he came undone fully, bucking hard against my mouth.

"Mmm," he grunted, his lips pressed tightly together. He squirted his own cum into my throat.

I held it again and shimmied up to a smiling Tavian. When he opened his mouth, I trickled Zared's cum inside.

"Mmm, tasty," Tavian said around his mouthful.

He exchanged glances with Zared. I realised neither had swallowed. Not yet.

They rolled me over into my back. Zared, then Tavian trickled all of the cum back into my mouth. The combined taste of them both was divine.

I smiled and swallowed the delicious mouthful.

"Gods that was hot," Tavian said. "We should include Ryze, Vayne, and Cavan next time. It's probably the only way you get to taste Vayne's cum."

"Doesn't it all taste the same?" Zared asked.

I couldn't tell if he was curious or disbelieving.

"Not at all." Tavian propped himself upon his elbow. "It depends what a person eats or drinks, or whatever. Some are tastier than others, right Khala?"

"Right," I agreed. "You all taste delicious." How did I get so fucking lucky? Sometimes, I thought maybe the gods didn't hate me after all. How could they when I was surrounded by five incredible men?

"You should get some sleep," Tavian said. "I'm going to go and see what Ryze needs. Zared, stay with her and make sure she actually does rest." He slipped out of the nest and pulled on his clothes before he disappeared out the door.

Zared pulled me to him and kissed the top of my head.

"Are you really all right? It sounds like what you

went through was...traumatic. Vayne is a pain in the ass, but it would suck if he died. Especially if you were right there to see it. I know you, you'd never forget it."

"No, I wouldn't," I agreed. "I really am all right. It's just a little weird knowing I owe most of that to Hycanthe, of all people. I'm starting to realise she's not as bad as I thought she was. Although, both of us have grown up a lot since we left the temple. A lot has happened. So much has changed. My whole life is different."

There wasn't an aspect of it that wasn't touched in some way. Some bigger than others. "I never would have thought I'd end up here."

"With me?" he asked.

"I think that was inevitable," I replied. "The rest of it is slightly crazy." I stifled a yawn with my hand.

"Just slightly," he agreed. "Get some rest. I'll watch over you. You're safe now."

I snuggled into him and closed my eyes. It didn't take long before sleep claimed me the way my five men had.

Deep and satisfying.

13

CAVAN

I huffed a breath as I strode out of the portal.

The last time I was in the Autumn Court things didn't precisely go according to plan, to understate the case.

I didn't blame Khala for a moment for stabbing me, although it hurt like a bitch. No, that act was all Wornar's fault. Recalling what he did to her afterward, I fumed. I dearly wanted to rip off his head and shove it up his own ass. He would be dealt with, I'd make sure of that, but first I had something else to attend to.

I strode towards the palace, senses on alert. At first glance, it appeared nothing was different. Nothing amiss.

I knew full well by now looks could be very deceiving. My instincts told me to be careful. I was inclined to give heed to them.

It quickly became evident someone was following me. Likely more than one someone.

I didn't look back. They weren't making any effort to hide their presence. They may have intent, but they weren't ready to act upon it yet.

The guards at the gates knew me by sight. None made the slightest move to stop me from passing. That in itself was curious. Harel made it clear I wasn't welcome here. Either that changed or no one informed the guards.

No, something else was going on here. I had the unshakeable sensation I walked in on something.

Even more cautious, I stepped towards the doors that led into the palace. As before, the guards let me pass.

"This is fun, isn't it?" Tavian spoke behind me as he followed me in.

I kept my eyes forward. I should have guessed it was him. Ryze must have sent him after me.

"Have you come to assassinate Harel?" I asked.

"Officially? No." He hurried to catch up with me. "Unofficially, if a knife happens to find its way into his forehead, I don't think too many people will mind." He grinned over his shoulder at the guards.

None of them made a move to stop either of us.

Evidently I wasn't the only one they recognised on sight.

"You know a High Lord doesn't pay well when people aren't willing to die for him," Tavian remarked.

I snorted softly. "Perhaps they realise he's not worth losing their lives for. Aah, Daniek."

I presumed the courtier would be slithering around somewhere. He seemed to have a sense for gossip and trouble. I glanced at Tavian and wondered if he'd seen anything with his sixth sense, since the Court of Dreams was released. I'd ask him when I got a chance.

"High Lord Cavan," Daniek said in his nasally, ingratiating tone. "What a surprise. Are you still busy chasing fables?"

His question clarified two things. Harel was still in charge, and Daniek was still a dickhead. The latter would never change. The former...

"Why don't you be a good boy and tell your High Lord I'm here to see him?" I said.

Beside me, Tavian twitched. That small movement spoke volumes.

I put that information in the back of my mind and raised an eyebrow at Daniek. I owed him no explanation and we both knew it. The best he could hope for would be for Harel to let him sit in on our meeting, or tell him details afterwards. No doubt he'd be salivating for every one of them.

Daniek gave me a slimy smile and waved his hand toward the throne room. "Of course."

He started there ahead of us so he could open the door and announce us.

I'd let him have his moment of pretending he was important.

Harel sat on a plush armchair near the window. He seemed less than pleased to see us. The polite thing for him to do would be to rise and greet us.

He remained sitting.

"Dropping in unexpectedly is becoming an unfortunate habit," he told me. "Have you brought me another broken omega?"

I didn't have to look to know Tavian's hand was hovering over a knife. One word against Khala and he'd use it.

"The Winter Court's *Master of Assassins* has accompanied me to speak on behalf of High Lord Ryzellius," I said. In case Harel forgot who and what Tavian actually was.

He was unique, and in some ways sweet, but Tavian was very, very dangerous. I wasn't entirely comfortable with how much he seemed to enjoy killing, but that was merely one facet of him. One of a great many.

"Is Ryze too much of a coward to come himself?" Harel sneered. "Or is it too much effort to come and say he was wrong?"

"On the contrary," I said smoothly. "He's busy gathering together as many Fae as possible who can use magic. I myself have just been in the Summer Court, organising the omegas I've been helping for the last twenty years."

I needed to get back to them as quickly as possible, and get them all to the Winter Court. All of this nonsense was wasting precious time.

"The Court of Dreams has awakened and been released," Tavian said. "As we speak, they're on their way to attack the Court of Shadows."

Harel regarded him for a moment, then threw his head back and laughed. "I see you've been hit in the head too many times with Ryze's cock. Even if this was true, what concern would it be of mine? If they destroy each other, perhaps you'll stop coming to my court and talking about them." He clearly didn't believe a word we said.

"They have griffins and magic," I said steadily. "Do you think they'll stop at the Court of Shadows?"

"They absolutely won't," Tavian said. "The Summer and Winter Courts will be ready. What about the Autumn Court?"

"We'll be ready," another voice said behind me.

Harel's face turned a delightful shade of pink. He looked like he might explode.

"Illaria, you are exiled from this court, under punishment of death." His voice was high, barely controlled.

In spite of the pressure we were under, I wouldn't have missed this for the world.

Illaria strode past us, chin high. "I challenge your authority. I declare you no longer fit to hold the title of High Lord. I have come to assert my claim and take my place as High Lady."

Harel spluttered. "You've lost your mind. Guards, seize her and take her to a cell. She'll be executed within the hour." He glared at her like she was something he scraped off the bottom of his favourite, and most expensive, pair of shoes.

Believing they were related to each other was difficult. Sometimes, family was a group of people who came together, not necessarily those who were related.

"I bet she has daddy issues," Tavian muttered.

The guards didn't move. Not one stepped forward to take her arm. They remained by the door, watching. After a minute or two, they were joined by others. Those from the front doors and the gate. And others still, moments later. None made a move to do as Harel ordered.

Now Harel stood and spluttered. "How dare you?"

"I dare," she replied. She glanced at Tavian and me. "Will you witness the change of leadership?" Her gaze was unwavering and unapologetic. She was entirely prepared for this. Completely ready to step up and take her place as leader.

I had no authority over who led another court, no say in it. Perhaps it was past time that changed.

I nodded. "I bear witness to your claim as High Lady of the Autumn Court."

"On behalf of High Lord Ryzellius, I bear witness to your claim," Tavian said formally.

Harel looked outraged and scared. "You can't do this. I am High Lord here."

"Not anymore," Illaria said. She nodded to the guards. Four of them stepped forward immediately and surrounded him. Two gripped his arms and looked pleased to do it.

Harel struggled for a moment before he was forced away.

"To his credit, he didn't piss himself," Tavian remarked. "Yet."

I shook my head at his comment and turned to Illaria. "I have a feeling you've been planning this for quite some time." That would explain the lack of reaction from the guards. They were expecting something to happen and knew I'd be on their side if it did.

Illaria wouldn't have to pay them too much more to die for her. She'd be a much better High Lady than her father was High Lord. Although, he lowered the standard quite a bit.

She gave me an innocent smile. "Perhaps I have and perhaps I haven't. Now, you were saying something about the Court of Dreams? What can the Autumn Court do to assist?"

"You can start by arranging any alpha who can do magic to come to the Winter Court immediately," I said. This was the conversation I'd come here to have. Granted, it would have been easier without the time we'd already wasted. "And any omegas you can, if there are any Harel doesn't know about."

The expression on her face confirmed what I

suspected. There were indeed such omegas present. They'd done well to stay away from Harel's gaze.

"Consider it done," she nodded. "Fortunately, my father's unpopularity was far-reaching. Much more than he realised. The whole court has been waiting for this move. They might not have backed me, but the return of the two courts... Let's say they're happy to have someone more competent leading. As far as I'm concerned, the Summer and Winter Courts are welcome here anytime."

"And you're welcome at the Winter Court." Tavian grinned. He seemed to enjoy playing the part of the High Lord's emissary. He didn't even seem too disappointed the coup was, so far, bloodless. No doubt he would have jumped in with two feet if Illaria took the court by force.

"And the Summer Court," I agreed. "But I need to get back there." I glanced at Tavian.

"I'm coming with you," he said. "I've decided I like your portals just as much as I like Ryze's."

I raised my eyebrows at him, but nodded.

"I've already had the wards removed," Illaria said. "You should be able to portal out from here."

I admired her ability to organise quickly. She must have put years into this coup. Her timing was nothing less than impeccable.

"I already like you much more than Harel," Tavian told her. "If you need help executing him, let me know when we've dealt with the Court of Dreams. I'm only too happy to assist."

She laughed softly. "I suspect I will have many offers of help. If you'll excuse me, I have alphas and omegas to assemble. We won't be far behind you."

Before I could take a step, she put a hand on my arm.

"Do you have a plan to deal with Wornar?" She couldn't possibly have known what happened to Khala, but from the look in her eyes, she understood what the man was like.

I suspected it was first-hand experience, but I wasn't going to ask, especially not now. If that was the case, she'd be as eager to see Wornar with a knife in his chest as the rest of us.

"Thiron might have assisted us, but Wornar won't," I said.

"He wouldn't live long enough to say no," Tavian growled.

I glanced at him to acknowledge what he said, then looked back at her.

"We can't worry about him right now. When we've dealt with the Court of Dreams, then we'll deal with him." I was sorely tempted to take Tavian there to dispense with him right now, but we didn't have the time.

Not to mention that I suspected Khala would want to be there. She should have a say in what happened to him. If she wanted to wield the knife, I'd let her. None of her pack would stop her. If anything, we'd hold him down for her.

Illaria nodded and lowered her hand. "We'll see you in a few minutes."

I nodded in return.

Without another word, I opened a portal back home to the Summer Court and hurried through, Tavian on my heels.

14

KHALA

The scent of alpha and omega was almost overwhelming.

Until now, I had no idea how many of us there really were. Several hundred from the Winter and Autumn Courts, along with sixty former Silent Maidens and more alphas from the Summer Court.

We gathered in the yard outside the Winter Court Palace. Us and several contingents of archers. A few thousand more had swords on their backs and steely looks in their eyes.

Wherever their High Lord led, they would follow and fight.

"Are you ready?" Ryze laced his fingers through mine and kissed my temple.

"Is anyone truly ready for something like this?" I asked.

"They are." Tavian had a faraway look on his face. "I've been getting bits and pieces of visions all morning. Things keep changing. One keeps reoccurring, though. Patric telling Yala and me the time has come. Whoever's visions these are, they're not happy about any of this."

"Gavil," I said softly. "I don't know how, but I think somehow you're getting his visions." I quickly told them about him.

"He foresaw all of this," Ryze mused. "In his visions and in his lived experience. I wonder if he knows how it will all end."

"Badly for them," Cavan said confidently. "I wonder if he told them that and they ignored him." He looked sly.

"You're never going to let us forget that, are you?" Ryze asked.

Cavan smiled.

Ryze shook his head. "Get a portal open, man. We have a court to help."

Cavan smirked and opened a portal to the side of Nallis. He stood beside it, keeping it open while Vayne ordered his people to march through with him.

For someone who almost died a couple of hours ago, the army commander was looking surprisingly well. He was clearly tired, but he was too fucking stubborn to admit it. Not to mention the fact he wasn't going to sit out of a perfectly good, potential battle.

He gave me a quick kiss before he strode past and disappeared into the long tunnel to Nallis.

The alphas and omegas went next, followed by the former Silent Maidens. I walked with them, side-by-side with Hycanthe and Jezalyn. Rijal trailed along behind.

"Does anyone else think this is a bad idea?" Hycanthe asked.

"It's your court too," I pointed out. "Unless you can convince them to stop?"

"She would if she could," Jezalyn said. She gripped Hycanthe's hand tightly.

"Yes, I would," Hycanthe agreed. "Also, I take no responsibility for what they do. I had no idea I had anything to do with them."

"I know you didn't," I said gently. No more than Tavian did. Blood didn't always equate to influence.

"Be ready," someone shouted from up the front.

A rumble came from behind and I turned back to see Zared push his way through to me.

"I wish I could throw you over my shoulder and take you away from here," he said. He slipped his hand into mine.

"Funny, I could say the same to you," I said lightly. "I'm sure I could carry you if I had to."

He smiled. "I'd like to see you try. In fact, let's go back to the Winter Court and do that right now."

Before I could say no, he squeezed my hand. "I know you won't go back. You're as stubborn as I am. Maybe more so. Make me a promise though. Don't take any risks unless you have to. We've come too far for me to lose you now." His voice was choked with emotion.

"I won't do anything stupid if you don't," I told him. "I love you."

"I love you too." He kissed me quickly before we stepped out of the portal and onto the side of the mountain.

"The mist is gone." Jezalyn sounded astonished.

"I don't see any griffins," Hycanthe was equally surprised.

"They could be trying to find a way into the caverns," Zared suggested.

"I know where they are," Tavian said. He hurried over to me and took my hands. "I can see the vision. Can you see it too, through the bond?"

I felt for it and got a hazy image, but that was all.

"I don't know if it's enough to open a portal there," I admitted.

"Can you try?" Ryze asked.

I hadn't seen him approach, but the portal was already closed behind him. We all stood on the side of the mountain, a stiff breeze blowing on all of us.

"I— I suppose so," I agreed. What was the worst that could happen? I'd open it to another place instead. A place we didn't have to walk through to. I'd close the portal and we'd try something else.

"Good girl," Cavan said, coming up behind me.

"Isn't she?" Vayne was close on his heels.

All of that praise was going to go to my head if they weren't careful. I turned my face so they couldn't see me blush too hard.

I nodded and stepped away from them into a clear space. I formed the portal in the air in front of me and peeled away the veil.

On the other side was pure chaos.

A wide plateau was set into the side of the mountain. At one end, a doorway led inside.

At the other, at least two dozen griffins hovered. They'd discharged a number of their riders. The ones who remained on the back were raining lightning down on the doorway, trying to blast their way in.

Bodies lay here and there. Mostly with golden hair, but a couple with black. Vernissa must have sent some of her people out here when the griffins arrived. By the look of them, they'd received no mercy at all.

"This is the place the mist took us," Vayne said, peering over my shoulder.

"It's the place I saw in my first vision." Tavian sounded haunted. "The place I saw all the death and destruction."

"Death and destruction aside, that's where we're going," Ryze said. He waved everyone over before stepping through himself.

Cavan was half a heartbeat behind.

Tavian, Zared and I were right on their heels, followed by everyone else in neat, disciplined order. Each archer, each swordsperson, knew exactly their position. They kept a precise distance between themselves and their comrades. Half a metre. Down the centimetre by the look of it.

"Aim for the riders, not the griffins," Vayne shouted out.

Almost as one, the archers pulled out their bows, took aim and fired.

The Silent Maidens separated amongst the ranks, before loosing shots of fire at the griffin riders.

Cavan did the same, while Ryze used blasts of ice.

What looked like an icicle speared one of the riders straight through the heart. She didn't even have time to cry before she fell off her mount and landed on the ground below with a sickening thud.

"Fall back to the doorway," Vayne ordered. The message was clear. The Court of Dreams would get to the Court of Shadows past us. We weren't going down without one hells of a fight.

We all fired off shots of ice and fire, frost and flame, while ducking lightning and sudden, violent eddies of wind. Several of our people were struck, or swept off the plateau.

The smell of burning hair and flesh soon pervaded the air and turned my stomach.

One of the griffin riders landed a shot of lightning right in the centre of the archers.

"Cover them!" Vayne shouted.

The Silent Maidens used hand language to communicate across the plateau, before working together to form a shield of heat in front of the archers. That gave them time to regroup and reorganise their ranks.

The griffin riders battered at the shield until it finally collapsed. One of them narrowed his eyes and aimed at a group of Silent Maidens, who stood near the back.

Before he could gather enough magic to attack, I speared him through the eye with a shard of ice. He flew backwards off his griffin and was thrown heavily to the ground. The griffin, apparently freed of her obligation along with her burden, banked and flew off towards the top of the mountain.

Another griffin wasn't so lucky. He got caught in the middle of a blast of flame. His scream of agony while his feathers and fur burnt was one I'd hear for the rest of my life.

He veered away before he crashed down in a heap on the edge of the plateau. The gods only knew if he was alive or not.

The griffin riders retaliated with an attack on the centre of our lines.

"We only need to concentrate on those five," Zared said.

Without taking my eyes off the riders, I asked, "Which five?"

"The middle one, the two on either side and there's two more mixed in. They're moving in and out of the others. The rest aren't doing magic, they're just covering for those five. There were seven, but we've got two of them."

Seven was a peculiar number. And it wasn't right. It was eight. Gavil was the last one, but he wasn't using magic against us.

He and his griffin were in front of another, shielding them from attack. They'd barely managed to dodge flames several times. Gods, he must be terrified. After what he went through as a child, he was having to face what had to be his worst nightmare.

There was that number again, eight. Eight Silent Maidens per year. Three transitioned. If I had to guess, I'd say Gavil was born looking like a Fae.

"Three of them are alphas," I guessed. "We need to focus everything on them." I twisted and sighed frantically to the closest of my sisters. She turned and signed to the sister who stood near Vayne. She, in turn, spoke to him quickly.

He nodded and stepped amongst the archers. He barked another order.

As one, the archers turned their bows and loosed their arrows. Everyone standing on the plateau who could use magic aimed at those three alphas.

All three of them realised quickly what was

going on. Two of them were too slow to react. They were incinerated.

The third turned his griffin and tried to flee. He got maybe ten metres before he froze. Literally. He was encased in ice from head to toe. The griffin shuddered and bucked, eyes wide in terror. Her rider was thrown clear. He landed on the ground and shattered into a hundred frigid shards.

"What a way to go," Zared muttered.

Without the three alphas, the rest of the griffin riders fell into disarray. Some returned fire with their own bows, but most turned their griffins and scattered. In moments they'd disappeared, some to the top of the mountain, and some below.

Three remained behind. None with a bow or any other, visible weapon, apart from their beasts and those huge talons, and sharp beaks. Those could do inestimable damage in moments.

The lead rider raised a hand. A gesture of surrender, a plea for mercy. It was more than Vernissa's people got.

A rumble went through our ranks. I wasn't the only one who glanced at Vayne for orders.

"Hold!" Ryze shouted before the archers took aim again. "Fire if they move to attack further."

Vayne nodded for everyone gathered to do as ordered.

No one relaxed a muscle, but we watched and waited.

Eyes on us, the riders directed their griffins to land and slid down off their backs.

Gavil and two other omegas.

Gavil sank to the ground and covered his face with his hands. His whole body shook. He was clearly terrified. Scared both of the flames and of what might happen to him now.

Somehow, I'd make sure everyone understood what he was subjected to, and what he risked speaking to me back at the castle. The blame for today shouldn't fall on his shoulders.

The plateau fell into silence, broken only by the groans of injured archers and Silent Maidens. The air was thick with smoke. It stung my eyes, making them water.

The two female griffin riders stepped away from their beasts, hands raised to either side. Both looked stricken.

I knew that look. That was the same look I saw in the mirror after Wornar made me run Cavan's knife through his side. The look of someone who only did harm because they were ordered by an alpha.

"How did you know?" Zared asked softly.

"I didn't," I admitted. "I guessed based on the way Dennin and Ramela talked about omegas. They saw them as something disgusting. That seems to lead to people assuming it's all right to use them. Like they're nothing more than tools. They couldn't help the things they were made to do."

"Neither could you," he reminded me. "You still blame yourself though, don't you?"

I leaned against him and shrugged one shoulder. "I probably always will. Whether it's rational or not."

"It certainly isn't," he agreed. "I guess this is where we leave the leaders to sort shit out."

"If you don't mind, I want to be part of that," I said. "Those omegas are going to need all the help they can get."

J stayed close to Ryze and Cavan as they addressed Vernissa and Lyra.

The High Lady regarded the new omegas with undisguised scepticism.

Calm radiated from Lyra, as always, although her brows creased every so often. That was as rattled as I ever saw her.

The three omegas knelt on the stone floor, Gavil in between the two women. He hadn't said a word since he slipped off his griffin.

Instead, a golden haired Fae with her hair in several braids spoke for the other two.

"You say you were given no choice," Ryze asked. He paced back and forth in front of them, keeping himself between them and Vernissa. Not so the High

Lady couldn't see, but to protect. An alpha protecting omegas. No one in the room missed what he was doing.

The omegas seemed grateful as well as forthcoming.

The woman, who said her name was Saminta, nodded eagerly. "High Lord Dennin ordered Patric to give us an alpha-order. As soon as the bubble was gone we were to take our griffins and come here to attack the Court Of Shadows. The moment Patric was shattered, the order stopped. We were free to choose. We choose not to fight against our fellow Fae. Especially omegas."

Both she and Betha, the other female omega, didn't seem surprised to learn the Court of Shadows was led by one.

"You knew that would happen," Cavan said softly to me.

"I hoped it would," I said. "It was Zared who realised we needed to focus our offence."

Before that, we were concentrating on defending the doorway into the caverns. No doubt I wasn't the only one who was intimidated by the presence of the griffins in the first place. If all of the riders could do magic, we'd be dead right now.

"If it didn't, we would have dealt with them," I

added. "There was no way to know the rest would leave once Patric was gone."

"Without anyone to do magic, they had only their griffins and regular weapons," Cavan said. "Against all of those former Silent Maidens, they wouldn't have stood a chance."

I reached for his hand and laced my fingers in his. "All of that work over all of those years—"

"Was worthwhile," he finished. "The eradication of Patric and the other alphas. And Yala too, from what I gather. Without them, we might not have got the upper hand in time. Although, we do have you."

"And you. And Ryze." I glanced over at Cavan and smiled. "But you're right, we needed them too." Out of sixty, we lost five. And as many archers.

"Can we expect the Court of Dreams to come after us again?" Ryze asked.

"The Court of Dreams is no more," Saminta said. "Outside the griffin riders, our numbers were few. Those who existed, the majority resided in the castle and the surrounding outbuildings. When the mist caused the earth to shake, most were lost. The attack on the Court of Shadows was a last effort to annex the court and save ours."

Vernissa sat forward. "Only a couple of hundred of you remain?"

Saminta nodded, her expression sombre. "That is correct, High Lady. We are at your mercy."

I caught a glimpse at the expression on Rijal's face. He stood near the wall, watching the proceedings intently.

He was clearly surprised to see omegas on their knees, much less supplicants to his mother. In some ways, he was like a child. Innocent of the world around him. He reminded me a lot of myself.

Vernissa sat back and glanced at Lyra. "I've long wanted to see the Court of Dreams at its end, but I find myself conflicted. Now Ramela and Dennin have gone, perhaps there is no need for animosity. Did they have an heir?"

"Yala was their heir." It was Betha who responded. "They have no other."

I glanced over to Tavian, who stood near Illaria. She'd arrived right after the battle was over and insisted on watching the proceedings.

"They may have another," I said. I nodded to Illaria to explain.

She told everyone what she told me about the High Lord visiting Tavian's mother and her becoming pregnant.

Tavian looked amused but not surprised. I should have known he already knew.

Saminta looked over to him. "I apologise, but the succession may only pass through the female line."

He grinned. "That's all right, I didn't want to be High Lord anyway. Being in a pack with two of them is plenty. May I make a suggestion?" Before anyone could tell him he couldn't, he continued. "What we need is someone with the blood of the Court of Dreams, right? Someone who understands how it feels to be an outsider. Someone with intelligence and compassion. Someone who isn't going to start any further antagonism towards omegas or alphas. Someone who doesn't take shit from anyone."

Slowly, dramatically, he raised his hand and pointed right at Hycanthe.

"What the fuck?" She stared at him like he was out of his mind. "Me?"

"Why not you?" Jezalyn asked proudly. "You're all of those things and more. I can't think of anyone better."

Neither could I. Tavian was right about her. The court was going to need someone strong to guide them and settle everyone back into their new lives. If anyone could do that, it was her.

"We approve of this arrangement," Saminta said after a quick, quiet few words with Betha and Gavil. She lowered her head. "High Lady Hycanthe."

"That's not going to go to her head at all," I said out of the side of my mouth.

Cavan chuckled. "Were you hoping it would be you?"

I snorted. "Fuck no. I have enough to deal with without leading a scattered court."

"A wise Fae once said the best person to lead is the one who is reluctant to do so," he said. "Someone who isn't merely concerned with their own ambition."

"So not someone like Harel or someone like Wornar," I said dryly.

"Definitely not," he agreed. "Although, now I think about it, I'm not sure Ryze or I fit that description either." He shrugged, seemingly unconcerned.

"Maybe that Fae wasn't that wise after all," I remarked. "Personally I'd suggest the best leader is someone who isn't an asshole."

Cavan hummed his agreement. "That is wise indeed. I'm thinking of suggesting we form a council of High Lords and Ladies, so we can make decisions together, instead of acting against each other when there's no need to do so. The first topic of conversation should be making that rule. No assholes."

"That's the smartest thing I've heard all day," Vayne commented. He'd walked up to us in time to hear. "Can we eradicate all assholes, not just the ones who lead?"

"You'd have to decide on the definition of asshole first," I said. "I suspect that might cause more trouble than it solves."

"Not if you appoint me judge of who is an asshole and who isn't," Vayne said. "I'm an excellent judge of character."

"Until recently, you thought I was an asshole," Cavan pointed out.

Vayne grunted. "Yes, well... We all make mistakes. I'm a big enough man to admit to mine."

We turned back to the proceedings as Vernissa stood. "I'm satisfied we've settled the matter of the Court of Dreams. We have two further matters to discuss. The presence and subsequent absence of the mist, and the matter of the returning of land to the Court of Shadows."

"The mist lifted from here the same time it lifted from the Court of Dreams?" I asked.

"As far as anyone can tell it did," Cavan agreed. "No one thinks that's a coincidence."

"Right, but the mist was around here for years, and only around the Court of Dreams for a matter of hours," Vayne said.

"Also probably not a coincidence," Cavan mused.

"How many years?" I asked.

"Around twenty," he said. He leaned back and looked at me. "About as long as you've been alive."

"And Hycanthe, and Jezalyn," I said. "And the gods know how many others. They were there along with me."

"The mist took them there," Vayne said. "It made sure you and Hycanthe were in the same place. It protected this place all those years. It kept out people like Ryze. And Ramela and Dennin."

"That doesn't mean it has anything to do with me," I said. Until I spoke, I didn't realise the room had fallen silent and everyone was listening.

"I figured you had Court of Shadows blood," Hycanthe pointed out. "I was right about that."

"How is that possible?" I directed the question to Cavan. "My mother was from the Summer Court. My father was—"

"Part human," Cavan finished for me. "He looked human, but he was half Fae. He must have been. He wasn't an alpha or an omega, so he didn't transition. I'd always thought he looked younger than he was. I should have realised it sooner."

"So one of my grandparents was from the Court of Shadows," I said slowly. "I never met my grandfather. My grandmother said he died before I was born."

The memory was vague, like most of my memories of those days. Just a few words I'd long since accepted as truth. Only now I realised they weren't.

My gaze drifted around the room before settling on Rijal.

"He didn't die, did he? The reason you always want to stay close to me is because you're my grandfather."

He started to sign, but Vernissa cut him off.

"You may speak," she said sharply.

He sighed. "I wanted to see the sun." His voice was gravelly and choked with emotion. "We fell for each other. Her parents and my mother did not approve. When she became pregnant, they forbade me from seeing her ever again. Whenever one of our people would go above, I'd ask them to check on our son. When he was born and looked human, they stopped going. It seemed better for him to get on with his life without knowing what he was."

His eyes were glazed. "But then when I saw you, I knew. You look like her."

Vernissa was visibly unimpressed, but this was clearly an old transgression. One she'd more or less come to terms with. Was this part of the reason her people weren't allowed to fuck each other? Because it created more problems than it solved?

To think a man who looked no older than me was my grandfather was strange. That would take some time to get my head around. Hopefully we'd get a chance to sit down and get to know each other.

"So you're the High Lady's great-granddaughter," Vayne remarked. For some reason, he seemed to find that funny.

Zared gave me a long glance. "Is there any way to find out if someone is part Fae?"

"You're talking about yourself?" Tavian asked him gently.

Zared shrugged. "It seems like something a man should know about himself. If Khala's father was half Fae and never knew, he's not going to be the only one, is he?"

Tavian smiled. "Unlikely. A lot of us struggle to keep our cocks in our pants."

Zared snort-laughed. "I noticed," he said without a hint of accusation or condemnation. "Anyway, is there?"

It was Lyra who answered. "There is, but we have a more important issue to resolve first. The matter of our land."

Vernissa nodded. "Yes. That must be resolved."

"We will speak to the King of Fraxius on your behalf," Ryze said. "However, I must remind you I have no say." He cocked his head. "Although, you know there's land available where the Court of Dreams were hiding."

"That land belongs to them and their griffins," Vernissa said. "I'm sure High Lady Hycanthe agrees."

Before Hycanthe could say anything, Vernissa continued. "We want our own lands. That way, both courts can thrive and return to their former glory."

Ryze gave her a bow. "We'll see what we can do." He didn't look confident, but somehow, one way or another, we'd find a solution to suit everyone.

"This isn't Fraxius," I remarked as I stepped through the portal into the sitting room in the Winter Court Palace.

"No it's not," Ryze drawled. "I made the arbitrary decision that we all needed a rest first. For one thing, we all smell like smoke. Except Vayne, he smells like feet."

"I fucking do not," Vayne protested. "I smell like good, honest sweat and blood. I smell like a warrior."

"Yes, you do," Tavian told him. "You smell like a warrior who is outnumbered by a pack that largely consists of High Lords and High Ladies." He grinned.

Vayne stuck his middle finger up at him. "You're not a High Lord. You and Ryze are trying to make me add you to my list of assholes."

I stepped up behind him and wound my arms around his neck. I kissed his cheek.

"None of you are assholes." They would never stop needling each other. I liked that they were close enough to tease each other and not get offended about what the others said. They pretended at offence, but that was all it was. A game between brothers.

"By rest, you mean..." Vayne grabbed my hands and pulled me around to face him.

"A bath and a nap," Ryze said. "Maybe with a few orgasms in the middle."

"That was what I thought." Vayne grabbed my ass and lifted me until I wound my legs around his hips. He brought his lips to mine and kissed me, deep and demanding.

He carried me like that all the way to my room and into the bathroom. He lowered me to the floor and I found myself surrounded by my entire pack.

All of the bonds felt close and warm. Like a blanket.

They helped me and each other out of their clothes and we all washed each other. Soap and water and wash cloths were everywhere, making the floor and each other slippery.

"Isn't that interesting?" Tavian remarked as he

washed my back and Zared's at the same time, a cloth in each hand.

I looked in the direction he nodded, to see Ryze swiping a cloth down Cavan's back. Both of their cocks were half erect.

"That's going to feature in my fantasies for a while," Tavian remarked.

I smiled. "Mine too." The air temperature rose suddenly.

Ryze and Cavan both turned to us and raised their eyebrows. They turned to each other.

I couldn't have been the only one holding my breath, waiting to see what they'd do. I didn't let it out until their lips met, lightly at first, then more deeply.

"Gods, yes," Tavian sighed.

I murmured my agreement. My whole body throbbed watching them kiss.

Ryze's hand slipped down to circle Cavan's cock. He slowly drew it up to his balls and back down to his tip.

Cavan groaned.

Vayne grabbed a towel and started to dry the front of me, then dropped to his knees with a faint splash. He parted my legs with his hands and flicked his tongue over my clit.

It was my turn to groan.

Tavian helped Zared to dry off and dropped to his knees. He curled the fingers of one hand around Zared's cock and cupped his balls with the other.

Zared groaned and pulled me over close enough so he could kiss me while Tavian and Vayne licked and sucked both of us. Between that and the sound of Ryze and Cavan's mouths on each other's, my whole body was on fire.

I rocked my hips, bucking against Vayne's mouth. He reached around to squeeze my ass, pinching every now and again. He gave me an especially tight pinch.

I gasped in a breath before I came. My orgasm pounded through me like thunder, hot blood racing through my ears. I arched my back and cried out.

Vayne lifted his face and, on a signal from Tavian, lay back on the wet tiles. Tavian and Zared lowered me, carefully sliding me down onto Vayne's thick cock.

"Lean forward," Tavian told me. He grabbed some lubricating oil and dipped his fingers inside before pressing them into my ass. His fingers stretched me, making me ready before he slid his cock inside my ass.

My eyes widened at the feeling of two cocks

inside me at the same time. It soon became a third, when Zared stood beside me and tapped on my lips with his.

"Open your mouth," he said.

I opened eagerly and let him slide his cock between my lips. After a few thrusts, all three men and I got a rhythm of sucks, licks and smooth strokes.

"Gods, you feel so fucking good," Tavian groaned. "You too, Vayne. I can feel your cock inside her."

Vayne grunted in response, but kept his eyes closed and pushed up into me.

"Oh my gods," Zared breathed.

I looked up and saw him with his gaze behind me. My hand on his cock, I lifted my mouth off him and looked over my shoulder.

Ryze was behind Tavian, the bottle of lubricating oil in his hand. He gave me a smile and prepared Tavian the way Tavian had prepared me.

Cavan stepped over to the other side of me. I curled my fingers around his cock and licked and sucked his tip before drawing him all the way down to the back of my throat.

Tavian stiffened for a moment and groaned. "Fuck yes." When Ryze thrust into him, he pushed

Tavian deeper into my ass. His momentum knocked me forward onto Vayne.

Ryze set the pace for all of us, thrusting slowly while I alternated between Cavan and Zared's cocks, my hands around their lengths the whole time.

The pressure built inside me again until I thought I might burst. I came for a second time, and a third.

That stole an orgasm from Vayne, who thrust up into me harder and faster before he shouted my name to the ceiling. He gritted his teeth and groaned long and low, the intensity of his orgasm flooding through the bond.

Tavian came next, deep strokes stilling as he spilled himself into my ass. Through the bond I felt a perfect, tight heat, and the delicious sensation of pure bliss that lasted before he finally floated back down to earth.

Ryze followed a moment later. I couldn't see him but I felt him too, the bond was full of emotion as well as bliss.

This wasn't just sex to him, this was about him giving everything to his pack. To our pack. Something he'd never had before. Something that made him feel complete. Content. Even more than being a High Lord, his place was here. He could have been a farmer or an executioner and still he would have belonged to us.

Our connection told me all of that and more.

Zared quickly followed Ryze, coming while his thick cock was almost down my throat.

"That's it. Suck me harder," he panted. "Gods, yes, yes, yes."

A squirt of hot cum blasted out of him and into the back of my mouth. It flooded my mouth with the smooth, salty taste. I held it there. Forced myself not to swallow. Instead I turned to Cavan and sucked him harder, my fingers massaging his balls.

I looked up at him to see him watching me.

"Good girl," he crooned. "Hold his cum. Wait for mine."

I sucked and licked him harder, grazed my teeth up and down his length and forced myself not to swallow. It took all of my focus. Everything else in the world disappeared except my mouth and his thick, throbbing cock.

His hips moved, driving him almost all the way to his knot. The tip of his cock was swimming in Zared's cum and the warmth of my mouth.

He grunted and thrust harder, fucking my mouth with even strokes.

I reminded myself to breathe as he came, spilling

another half a mouthful of hot cum down my throat. It quickly mingled with the first, making a ball of hot liquid in the back of my mouth.

"Good girl," he said breathlessly. "Take every drop but don't swallow." He went on thrusting until his cock lost some of its hardness. Only then, he slid out of my mouth and took half a step back.

"Such a good girl." He kissed my brow, then turned my face to Tavian as he slid his cock out of my ass. He manoeuvred me until our mouths met. I kissed Tavian, but kept my mouthful where it was for now.

I broke off the kiss and slipped off Vayne's cock.

Looking around deliberately, I stood and wound my hands around the back of Ryze's neck. I pressed my mouth to his and squirted my mouthful between his lips.

He swished his lips from side to side as though tasting a fine wine. "Mmm." He eyed all of the other men speculatively.

Vayne shook his head, but Zared, Tavian and Cavan simply gazed back. Each with an expression of curious interest on his face.

I had to give it to them, they were adventurous. Lucky for me, because so was I.

Finally Ryze stepped over to Cavan and pressed

his mouth to his, passing on the tasty mouthful to the other High Lord.

I wasn't sure how Cavan would react, but he did the same as Ryze, tasting and appraising before he grabbed Tavian by the back of his head and slammed his mouth down onto his.

"Delicious," Tavian said, licking his lips. He turned from Cavan to Zared, tipping Zared's head back and dribbling the cum inside.

I thought Zared would swallow it, but he didn't. He took his turn in tasting before he grabbed me and gave it back where it started. Pressing the warm, wet ball into my mouth.

I accepted it, even licking his lips to make sure I got all of it.

By now, it tasted different, but no less delicious than it started. I smiled at all of them and swallowed it down. Every last drop.

"Well, that was hot," Tavian remarked. "Ryze, I thoroughly enjoy your idea of a rest. We should definitely all *rest* more often."

"We absolutely should," Ryze agreed. He stepped over to me and cupped the back of my head in his hands.

"You are amazing. After everything you've been through since we met, most would be ruined. But not you. You're stronger, tougher and even more beautiful." His throat bobbed with emotion. "I need you to know I love you."

"I love you too," I told him. I kissed him, putting all of my emotion and warmth into it.

I broke off and turned to Cavan. "I love you too."

He smiled. "And I love you."

It felt good to say that to them. I wasn't sure if I'd get the chance to do it.

"I hate to interrupt," Tavian said. "But I just want to say I love Ryze. I told Khala and Zared, but I never told you. I thought it might make things awkward, but I want you to know."

Ryze grabbed his arm and pulled him over. "I love you too." They kissed each other lightly, tentatively at first.

Seeing them like that warmed my heart and my body.

Vayne and Zared both slipped an arm around me and leaned into me.

"It's like one big happy pack," Vayne remarked. "We managed to avoid full-blown war and everyone loves everyone else."

"Does that mean you love Zared?" I asked.

Zared leaned and looked around me to him, his eyebrows raised.

"I love him like a brother," Vayne said with a grunt. "Just like the rest of them. I don't want to touch you, but I don't mind your company once in a while."

"Thanks," Zared said sarcastically. "You too. I guess we're back to training when we return from Fraxius?"

"Definitely," Vayne agreed. "We don't want you getting soft."

Zared scoffed. "I could never get soft. I could get hard again though." He grinned.

While Ryze and Tavian kissed, Zared, Vayne and Cavan slipped off with me to my nest.

"This is going to be strange." I gripped Zared's hand and found it as sweaty as mine.

"Going to Havenmoor was weird enough. Then, I was thinking about seeing you. I wasn't thinking so much about being surrounded by humans again. Going to Phikus, knowing they'll only see me as Fae..."

"And they'll only see me as a human in the company of Fae," Zared said.

His tone made me turn to him. The expression on his face was sad, reflective.

"You're hoping to discover you're part Fae, aren't you?" I asked gently.

"Wouldn't you?" he asked back. "Think about

what it might mean for both of us. I'd age slower. I might even live almost as long as you. We could grow old together. Before any of this happened, that was all I wanted for us. Now..."

He sighed. "I know it never would have happened. You were always going to become who you are."

"Why do I get the feeling you're saying goodbye to me." I cocked my head at him. "If you want to stay in Phikus, I won't stop you." Tavian might try, possibly the rest of the pack as well, but it had to be his choice.

"Not a chance," he said easily, immediately. "Whatever happens, you're stuck with me. I feel like..." He frowned.

"What do you feel like?" I prompted gently.

"When I first came here to the Winter Court, I felt angry. I wanted to force you to go back with me. Even after you changed. I wanted to be anywhere but here amongst the Fae. But now, I know they aren't that different to any of the humans in Ebonfalls. It's taken me a while, but I know it now. In most cases, they're better than anyone there."

"Here, they ask for permission to strap my ass," I said with a smile. "That seems like a dozen lifetimes ago. I watched Hycanthe have her choker removed before me. Now she's literally High Lady of the Court of Dreams. Tyla is living her best life, enjoying what Havenmoor has to offer. And I'm the great-granddaughter of the High Lady of the Court of Shadows."

"And I'm a part of your pack," he said. "And somehow I have two Fae lovers." He didn't elaborate on any potential for him to form a relationship with Ryze or Cavan. There was plenty of time for that.

"But you wish you were Fae too," I said.

I hesitated for a moment. Frowned. "I wonder if I could do what Lyra says she can. In theory, I have some of the same kind of magic as she does. I should be able to remove stone from people if you get stuck again."

It hadn't occurred to me at the time that might have been possible. If it was, what else might I be able to do?

"I trust you," he said without reservation. "It can't hurt to try."

Those sounded like famous last words to me, but I took him farther aside from where the others were getting ready to go to Fraxius. Ryze, Tavian and Vayne were arguing some point about how armed they should be. Cavan was watching on and adding a word here or there. They didn't notice us move away.

Zared sat on a chair near the window. I knelt beside him.

"I'm not really sure what it is she does," I admitted. "When I brought those fish back to life, I felt... under their skin."

I hadn't given it much thought until now. Too many other things had occupied my time and thoughts. Now I thought about it, I realised I could have sliced off a layer or two.

"I'll try to take a peek."

He nodded. "I said I trust you. I know you're not going to kill me. And if you do, you know how to bring me back to life, right?" He gave me a smile that was now tentative.

I almost backed away and told him no, I wouldn't even *try* to do anything to him.

I didn't because he wanted this, and because if I stepped away now, he'd ask Lyra to try instead. He'd risk everything to know the truth.

I took a deep breath and put a hand on his muscular bicep. His rock hard muscles gave me reassurance. If he trusted me, then I could trust myself.

I grabbed hold of what magic I could get. Now the mist was gone, I could access more than ever.

Cavan surmised the mist was somehow created by me from my magic. It was a part of me. Now it was gone, I had less of a drain on the rest of me.

I delved into Zared, worming the magic under his skin.

He shivered lightly. "That tickles."

I smiled. "It's good to know I can tickle you from the inside and the outside. I know how much you love being tickled." About as much as I did. Not at all.

"Don't make me regret letting you do this," he said in a mock growl. Even speaking playfully like that, he got my pulse racing.

I never could resist his growls.

I delved in further, trying to discern what might make him Fae and what would clarify that he was all human. I looked for a hint of magic, but didn't find one. I didn't expect to. I wouldn't have found one in Tavian either, so that was far from an indication.

I pushed a little further, until I reached a place inside him that seemed familiar. Strangely so. I couldn't figure out what it was at first.

"What the fuck?" I whispered.

"No offence, but that's not what a man wants to hear when you're literally under his skin," Zared said softly. "I'd prefer something along the lines of, 'oh my gods, he's hot on the inside too.'" He grinned.

"Which is undeniably accurate." I hadn't known Ryze approached until I heard him speak near me. The rest of the pack was close now too.

"Definitely accurate," Tavian agreed.

"You two are out of your minds," Vayne told them. "I'm clearly the best looking under my skin."

"Says you," Tavian said.

I shook my head slightly at their banter. Only they would argue over who was the best looking on the *inside*.

Cavan crouched down beside me and brushed his fingers over the side of my neck. "What is it? Is he part Fae?"

"I..." I considered a response while I delved a little deeper. "I think he might be... But, I don't know, there's more to it than that."

Zared twitched. "What do you mean?" He sounded scared, but didn't pull away.

I looked over to Cavan. "When Dalyth put that block on his mind—"

"What did she do?" Zared sounded frantic now. His heart started to beat faster.

"Nothing," I said quickly. "This isn't about her.

This is about the block. I thought it was something —I don't know—unnatural and intrusive."

"But now?" Cavan asked. "What do you think it was?"

"Now I think maybe she used..." I thought about it for a few moments longer.

"She used his body against him, I guess you could say. Like the alpha-order you put on me to ignore all other orders, and to put aside what...*he* did to me. The order acts on natural instincts. I needed to forget and move on, for my own sanity. Without that, I'd still be a mess. But the orders don't always follow what an omega really wants."

"He overrode what was best for you. His order forced your omega instincts to respond to him," Tavian said gently.

I tried not to shudder. "Something like that," I agreed. "When an omega goes into heat, those instincts take over. He used those against me."

"Are you saying I *wanted* to forget you?" Zared asked.

I glanced up his face. "No. You said yourself when you got here, you wanted to leave. You were under a lot of stress and pressure. She took that and used it against you."

"That makes sense, but what does that have to do with whatever you've found now?" Ryze asked.

My gaze went over to him. "All we want in life is to belong. We don't want to be the odd one out."

"I prefer to be the odd one *in*," Tavian said. "It's much more fun that way."

I smiled at him briefly. "Do you remember the border patrol?"

"The young Fae male with the human ears?" he asked. "I remember that. He definitely would have been an odd one out."

Of course, Ryze couldn't resist saying, "That's the Summer Court for you."

Cavan rolled his eyes.

"I think those of us who are part Fae have the same kind of block Dalyth put on Zared's mind. It keeps us from looking different to those around us. That particular Fae either had a smaller block or none at all." I was guessing here. Unless there were others like him, we'd never know.

Cavan nodded slowly. "You think when you went into heat, the block was destroyed? That's what made you transform."

"That makes sense," Tavian said. "It had to be something that was triggered off. A block is as good a word for it as any."

"Are you saying Zared has a block like that?" Vayne asked bluntly. Trust him to get right down to the point.

"That's what it feels like," I agreed. "It feels familiar because I had one the same."

"Wait a minute, are you saying that if you take the block away, I'll transform?" Zared asked. He looked hopeful. And terrified.

"I'm not sure," I admitted reluctantly. I didn't want to get his hopes up and then dash them again. He'd be devastated. "It might take something like a mating heat, or it might kill you."

Silence hung in the air, thick and heavy.

"I'm guessing a mating heat is out of the question," Tavian remarked.

"He's definitely a beta," Ryze said. "So yes, it is out of the question. Unfortunately. Three omegas would be even more fun."

Zared's face swivelled towards him, then back to me.

"This isn't something you have to decide right now," Ryze said. "That block has been there this long, it can stay for as long as you need, if not forever. Which, if Khala is right, is longer than we initially anticipated."

That was certainly something to thank the gods for.

"Have you ever heard of anything like this?" I asked Cavan.

"To be honest, I don't think anyone has thought to look," he admitted. "We knew to watch for alphas and omegas, but beyond that... No. Very few humans would have allowed themselves to be delved with magic like this. It's possible this is more common than we know."

I nodded slowly. He was right about humans not letting Fae in, in this way. I wouldn't have let anyone delve into me.

"Do it," Zared said softly. "I want you to try to take the block out now."

"Are you sure?" Tavian asked.

"I'm absolutely sure." Zared nodded firmly. "I want this. Do it."

I hesitated for longer than a few moments. I appreciated his faith in my abilities, but I was a little short on faith in myself.

"If this is what you really want..."

He twisted his upper body and took my hands in his. "This is what I want. I want to be one of us in every way that counts."

"You are one of us in every way that counts," I

told him. "Just because you don't have pointed ears—"

"It makes me the odd one out," he said.

"You still belong," I argued.

"Do I? Didn't you just say we have a block to make sure we do belong? Mine was to make sure I belonged with other humans. That's not my life. I don't need it. I need *this*. I need *you*. I want you to do this for me. *Please*." He begged me with his eyes.

I exhaled softly. "All right, I'll try, but it may not work. It might just be a part of you. If it is, if nothing happens, I love you. No matter what you look like. No matter..."

I shook my head. "No matter what."

"I love you too," he replied. He sat back in the chair and put his head back. "I'm ready."

"Wait," Tavian said. He stepped over and kissed Zared on the mouth. "I love you."

"I love you too," Zared told him. He waited until Tavian stepped back and closed his eyes.

"I'm ready."

18

KHALA

I almost told Zared no, but the look on his face convinced me to close my own eyes and delve in deeper still. The block was different to the one in his mind. He was born with this one. It was as much a part of him as his eye colour or his stubbornness. I couldn't change either one of those even if I wanted to, which I didn't.

Fortunately, the block wasn't in his mind. His mind was a complicated place, I didn't want to touch that again if I didn't have to.

On the other hand, it was close to his heart. I'd have to go carefully.

"Tell me if this doesn't feel right," I said. "I'll stop straight away if it does."

He murmured his agreement and sat completely still. I suspected he was holding his breath.

Like I had with the one in his mind, I worked magic around the block, testing and teasing to see if it would come away.

The moment my magic touched it, it flinched. It leapt onto my magic, completely untangling itself from him.

"What the fuck?" I let out a short cry of surprise. The block was completely gone.

Zared's heart beat rapidly a few times, then stopped entirely.

"Fuck," I whispered.

Over the pounding in my ears, I heard Tavian frantically calling out Zared's name.

"He's not breathing." I couldn't tell who said that. I could hardly think past my own panic.

"Khala, take a breath," Cavan said. "Stay calm. You know what to do."

"Yes, you do," Ryze agreed. "Khala, you can do this. You have the magic of the gods inside you."

His words echoed around my mind.

The magic of the gods...

The magic of the...

The magic of...

The magic...

The...

I grabbed every bit of it I could and worked heat into Zared's heart. Not hot enough to burn, but hot enough to work its way inside and pump for him. Once. Twice.

I put air into his lungs to inflate them. In. Out.

Don't you dare die on me, I silently begged. *I need you.*

If I killed him, I'd never forgive myself. For the rest of my life, I'd wish I hadn't told him about the block. I should have kept my lips shut. I should have—

Zared gasped in a breath. His heart started to pound on its own.

A moment later, everything started to shift. His whole body started to change from the inside out.

I pulled my magic free of his body before it was consumed.

His back arched against the chair. Eyes shot open. He tilted his head back and cried out in pure agony.

His face became pale. His chin grew longer, more pointed. His ears lost their roundness. His eyes changed from human, to the Fae catlike shape. Even his hair seemed to grow longer. His body became slender and lithe, if just as muscular.

When I thought he couldn't take any more pain, he slumped down, covered in a sheen of sweat. He panted heavily out his nose and groaned.

He sat like that for a good few minutes, catching his breath. Eventually, he looked up, looked over at me.

"That sucked."

I smiled, relieved at hells to hear him speak. "How do you feel?" I asked.

That was shorter and less dramatic than when I transformed. Potentially because of the way it happened. It wasn't a spontaneous change. Or an unexpected one.

He shrugged and ran a hand up his face and over his ear. "I feel... The same. I guess I don't look the same?" He poked a finger at the tip of his ear.

"You look even more attractive than you already did," Tavian told him.

He grabbed Zared's hand and pulled him to his feet. He tugged him over to a mirror on the wall. "See for yourself."

Zared stared at himself for what seemed like a lifetime.

I was about to ask him if he regretted letting me remove the block, when he said, "Tavian is right, I do look even more handsome." He grinned at his reflection.

I socked him on the arm. "You're just as handsome as you were."

"Yeah, but—" He turned around to face me. "I'm taller than you again."

I looked up at him and grimaced. "I knew I should have left you the way you were. Maybe I could try to put you back."

"Not a chance," he said lightly. "I'm one of us now. Inside and out."

"Fucking hells," Vayne growled. "I'm never going to hear the end of this from Ryze."

Ryze looked at him innocently. "I have no idea what you mean."

"Bullshit," Vayne spat. "You're probably already planning to replace me with him." He jabbed a finger in Zared's direction.

"I wasn't," Ryze said slowly. "But now..."

Cavan clapped Vayne on the shoulder. "If he tries to do that, you can always come and command my army. I could use someone with your experience."

Ryze looked outraged. "You do not have my permission to poach my commander."

Cavan responded with a sly smile. "Fine, I'll poach Zared."

Ryze pretended to splutter, while Tavian laughed. "You two are adorable together."

Cavan and Ryze both looked at him and rolled their eyes.

I shook my head at the lot of them and grabbed Zared's wrist. "I'm sure you want to get changed before we go to Phikus," I said. "You seem to have outgrown your clothes."

He glanced down at his pants, which were now a hand span too short. "Well, fuck, you're right."

Did I imagine it, or was his voice deeper? Sultrier? Holy gods.

He looked back up. "Any way of knowing which court I might have come from?"

It was Ryze who responded. "Judging from your hair and eye colour, and your tendency to be as grumpy as shit, I'd say you're from the Winter Court."

A smile slowly grew on his lips. "Hells, for all I know you could be my son. Would that be funny?"

"No," Zared stated. "Not even a little bit." He shot Vayne a dirty look when the army commander chuckled. "Fuck off."

"That's fuck off, *sir*, to you," Vayne told him. "I'm still your commanding officer. More so, now no one will question your presence in my army."

"I'm thinking of poaching him to finish his assassin training," Tavian said thoughtfully.

"Don't you start," Vayne growled.

Tavian grinned. He didn't even look slightly apologetic.

I shook my head at them all and pulled Zared away to hunt down a new pair of pants for him.

"Are you sure you're all right?" I asked. "It takes time to get used to looking and feeling different."

"I feel fine," he said. "Better than fine. My vision is clearer. My hearing is stronger. I bet if you made a wall of ice across the river, I could run as fast as any of you. Faster. I'll be quicker with a sword too. But—"

I wasn't surprised to hear him add that on. Of course there had to be a but somewhere in there.

"What is it?" I asked gently.

He pulled me into his room and closed the door behind us.

"Aren't you curious to know if my cock is as big as theirs now?"

I should have known that was the first thing he'd think of it. That might have been his motivation for wanting to change in the first place.

Men.

"Now you mention it, I might be a little curious," I said, giving him a sideways, cagey look.

"Good. Get on your knees and take him out." He crossed his arms over his chest and arched an eyebrow at me.

I smiled and lowered myself down onto the rug that lay on the floor. My eyes on his, I undid the front of his pants and eased them down.

I lowered my gaze and blinked a couple of times.

"Holy gods." He was longer and thicker than he was before. As I expected, he had no knot, but what he had was impressive as fuck.

"Suck me," he ordered. "I want to know how I feel in your mouth."

"Yes, sir." I gripped his length in my fingers and teased his thick tip with my tongue. I traced circles all the way around and tasted the pre-cum that leaked from his slit. I fastened my mouth around him and started to suck lightly.

He quivered. "This feels different too. More... sensitive. More... I don't know, just more. Gods, it feels so fucking good."

He tangled his fingers in my hair and drove me harder on and off his cock. His hips moved in rhythm with my sucks.

Eventually, he pulled me off him and drew me to my feet. "On my bed, now. I need to be inside you."

My whole body was throbbing with need. I

scrambled onto the bed, shedding clothes as I went. By the time I lay back on the mattress, I was naked and dripping wet.

He was just as gloriously naked as he stepped up to the side of the bed. He grabbed my ankles and dragged me down to him until I lay with my ass right on the edge. He locked my legs around his waist and impaled me on his heavy cock.

His lips dropped apart. "Gods, I didn't think it could feel better than you did before, but this is something else. So tight. So fucking good."

He stayed like that for a while before slowly thrusting into me, his eyes half closed as he took his time. He reached in between us to run his fingers over and around my clit.

"Do I feel good to you?" he asked. "Do I feel better to you than I ever did before?"

I groaned softly. "You feel incredible. You fill me so much. So fucking much." I rocked my hips gently, sliding myself across his fingers and letting my muscles milk his cock.

"I'm going to fill you even more," he said. "I'm going to fill you to the brim with my cum. That is going to be even better too. So much it's going to fill you until you overflow."

"Gods, yes please," I said breathlessly. "I'm going to come."

"Yes, you are. Come on my cock." He rubbed more deliberately now, slender fingers feeling even more incredible than they used to. Expertly bringing me to the edge and holding me there before I tipped all the way over into sweet oblivion. The world shattered into a million tiny lights before coming back together again.

He came a moment later, thrusting, driving hard into me, his teeth gritted. "Fucking hells, yes." He grunted and panted several times, groaning and grinding, drawing out every delicious drop.

Finally, he gasped and sagged, panting heavily before he caught his breath. "So fucking good," he whispered. "Fucking incredible."

He slowly slid out of me and gripped my knees. He held me like that, my legs spread wide, watching as his cum trickled out of my pussy. Letting go of one knee, he pressed his finger into the entrance to my pussy.

"Don't want it to dribble out too quickly."

He stayed like that for a few minutes before sliding his finger out and pressing it between my lips. "Suck."

I opened my mouth and sucked his finger,

tasting the combination of him and myself. Delicious.

"We're going to go to Phikus with the others. I'm going to enjoy knowing you're going to be sticky with my cum the entire time." He turned me slightly to the side and slapped my ass before stepping away. "We should hurry or they'll leave without us."

"They better not," I growled. But I jumped up and started to pull my clothes back on.

19

*Z*ared looked like the cat that got the fucking cream when he and Khala finally reappeared. She was still combing her fingers through her hair and patting it down into place.

Ryze grinned. "It's about time you two reappeared." No doubt, like the rest of us, he'd felt them screwing down the bond. "We were about to leave without you."

"No, you weren't," Zared said.

It would take some time to get used to the way he looked now. The asshole was taller than me, and wider too.

Luckily I had looks, brains and personality.

"Figures the first thing you'd do when you looked like the rest of us was fuck Khala," I told him.

"Because it's exactly what you'd do?" Tavian asked. He was busy checking all his knives were in place all over his body. If you didn't know him, you wouldn't think he had any, but he seemed to have found a way to carry ten of them. I got the impression his life's ambition was to see how many he could carry without looking armed. As life ambitions went, it wasn't a bad one, I supposed.

"Damn right it is," I agreed. I adjusted my sheath on my shoulder, making sure my sword was sitting right. Earlier in the day we had a conversation about whether we should go to Phikus unarmed, or at least without visible weapons.

I'd argued it was a quick way to end up dead. Fortunately, Ryze agreed. He wore his bow and quiver on his back, although Phikus was nestled beside a lake that meant Ryze's magic would probably do.

I suspected he was slightly jealous of Khala's apparent ability to use her magic anywhere. Only slightly jealous though. Ryze didn't really do feelings like that too often. Even Fae life was too short for that kind of shit.

I caught Cavan looking at Zared, in the corner of my eye. I turned towards him the same time Zared noticed his expression.

"What?" Zared asked.

Cavan inclined his head slightly. "I was thinking this might be easier if you still looked human."

"Too late for that," I pointed out. "If you thought it would be a problem, you should have said so before Khala did the thing she did." I wasn't going to pretend to understand how any of that worked.

"Do you think that would have changed anything?" He seemed genuinely curious.

"Not one thing," I said. "Once they were set on doing what they did, that's what they were going to do. Nothing you or I could do about that."

"Would you have tried to stop them?" Ryze asked him.

Cavan considered the question for a moment. "I'd be a hypocrite if I said I'd try to stop someone from transitioning, but it does raise some issues. How many are there like him who don't know it? Would they want to know? And how many Fae could change to look human? If they could, would they?"

"For the record, I don't want to know," I said. "And if I did, the answer is no. I like me just the way I am."

Khala stepped over to me and pressed the back of her knuckles against my cheek. "We like you just the way you are too. I love you just the way you are."

"Me too," Tavian said.

"Yes, yes, we all love Vayne as he is," Ryze said. "I think we should keep this to ourselves for now. It raises far too many questions we don't have time to answer. Same with Khala's ability to bring people back to life. I'd hate to be cynical and suggest people might want to abuse such an ability, but they might."

"They very much would," Cavan agreed. "Not to mention the fact if the humans knew the Court of Shadows had an ability like that, there's no chance they'd agree to share their land."

"I hope you have a backup plan," I said. "Because there's no chance they're going to agree to this."

"Maybe not," Ryze said, "but we have to try, if only so we can go back to Vernissa and say we did." Judging by the look on his face, there was no backup plan.

I sighed softly to myself. So far, the inevitable all-out war hadn't happened yet. Even with the griffins, the Court of Dreams didn't have the resources for it.

The Court Of Shadows, on the other hand, had a lot more people. They were also a lot more desperate. They wanted out of those caverns and I had a feeling there was nothing they wouldn't do to achieve that.

They also had the ability to encase people in fucking stone. I shuddered at the memory.

Ryze nodded to Cavan. "You're more familiar with the land around Phikus than I am. You might as well make the portal."

For once, no one turned it into a sexual innuendo. If that didn't speak volumes about the tension, nothing would.

Cavan checked his weapons, then opened a portal in front of us.

His portals were freaky as fuck, I have to admit. I felt like I was about to step through the flames into the depths of one of the seven hells.

Before anyone else could, I took Khala's hand and we stepped through together. I kept her a little behind me, in case we encountered something nasty on the other end.

As commander of the army, it was my job to make sure the other side was safe. As a member of her pack, I wanted to keep her close.

We stepped out on grassland that reminded me of the Court of Dreams, but without the castle. Although, since the court didn't have a castle anymore either, I looked around carefully, just in case.

No, this definitely wasn't the same place. For one thing, there was no hill. Nothing but flat farmland, with trees dotted here and there.

"It's pretty," she remarked. We moved aside to let the others step out.

"If dirt and cows are your thing," I remarked. "No running hot water. No decent taverns anywhere close." Nothing but wheat and corn as far as the eye could see.

"You prefer the city?" she guessed.

"Definitely," I agreed. "Don't get me wrong, this is nice, but it's...boring. I'd go as crazy as Tavian in half a day."

"Some would say you're already almost there." Ryze stepped out behind us.

I smirked at him.

"There's nothing wrong with being crazy," Tavian was on Ryze's heels. "Some people would say sanity is overrated."

"Are you those people?" Cavan asked. He closed the portal behind us.

Tavian grinned. "I'm certainly *one* of those people. If you all look deep inside yourselves, you'll find out you are too."

I grunted softly. "Speak for yourself. In fact, don't.

Let's get to Phikus and get this over with." I wasn't big on talking at the best of times. Ryze and Tavian would talk anyone's ear off if they got the chance. Mostly I tuned them out unless they had something interesting to say.

"How far is it?" Khala asked. She scanned the skyline and obviously came to the same conclusion I did. It must be a long way, because the land was so flat we'd see it if it wasn't.

"A few kilometres," Cavan said. "In that direction." He nodded. "Once we get to the road, we'll see humans. Especially ones with horses. By the time we arrive in Phikus, they'll know we're coming."

"We may not be welcome," I pointed out.

"It's very likely we won't be," Zared agreed. He seemed disconcerted to realise he really was one of us. He couldn't march into the city and have a pleasant chat with the king.

Granted, that was unlikely anyway. Kings and High Lords didn't seem to like it when people just turned up unannounced, expecting to see them. How they'd take it when a group of Fae turned up was anyone's guess. Hence that we were armed.

At uneasy times like this, I was glad people around me could use magic. Three of them could open a portal and get us the fuck out of here at a moment's notice.

Although, fighting people who lived in a place like this wouldn't be an even match anyway. They were farmers and shopkeepers. Regular humans, not soldiers. No doubt the king had guards around here somewhere, but they wouldn't be at the level of skill of the rest of us. Not to mention the speed and agility that came with being Fae.

"We'll deal with that when we arrive," Ryze said easily. He didn't seem even slightly concerned we'd be turned away. Then again, it was Ryze. He'd charm his way in.

I glanced over to Khala and shrugged. Keeping close by her side, I started walking.

"Phikus looks like a bigger version of Ebonfalls," Khala remarked. She appeared underwhelmed, to say the least. I wasn't sure what she was expecting, but it clearly wasn't this.

Personally, I wasn't surprised. Human cities seemed more focused on function than form. The buildings were timber and stone cubes, with windows in the side. Some had balconies, but most didn't. All of them were built three or four steps off the ground, with a small set of stairs leading up to a door.

Some of the buildings were painted white or green, but the paint was peeling off in chunks. In spite of that, they looked structurally sound. None of the fascia was cracked, or the corbels broken. Most of the windows were clean, including a couple of high transoms.

If nothing here looked like flowers, or leaves, or ice, at least they were well taken care of.

The largest building in the city was a castle nestled in the centre. It was smaller and less grand than the one in the Court of Dreams, but was other-wise strikingly similar. In spite of its simple design, it was clearly Fae built, and old. One of many aban-doned by the Court of Shadows when they went into hiding.

Chin raised, I walked through the streets with the others, ignoring the plentiful stares of humans as we went past. Mutters followed us as we went, but no one tried to approach us.

None of them dared.

Tave, being Tave, smiled and spoke to several of them as he went past.

"Lovely day," he called out to one of them. "Nice

flowers. I might have to come back and buy some." Pleasant greetings from a man who would cut their throats in a moment if he needed to. Of course, he'd also buy flowers from them.

I had a feeling he'd get much more enjoyment out of them if the petals were sprinkled with droplets of blood. No one ever said he wasn't fucked up.

Although, I was having these thoughts about him, so maybe we were as bad as each other.

The closer to the castle we went, the more the rumblings increased. In volume, in intensity and in barely suppressed aggression.

I kept my whole body tense and ready. I locked eyes with a few humans before walking past. If they thought about attacking us, they might think again. Sometimes, a little bit of fear went a long way.

"I have a bad feeling about this," Khala said. "Something isn't right."

"Something is definitely off," I agreed. "It's probably just that they don't like Fae here. They wouldn't see any of us very often." Unless one of the other courts visited more frequently than we did. The gods only knew what Harel used to get up to. Thiron either, for that matter.

"That could be it," she said slowly. "But I don't think—"

She was interrupted by the opening of the wide gate that led from the castle.

A contingent of Fae stepped out towards us.

At the front of them walked Wornar.

I froze completely. I couldn't have run if I wanted to, which I didn't.

I didn't know what I wanted to do more, punch him in the face or knee him in the cock. Maybe slice off his balls with a blunt knife and feed them to him.

The list was long and without any firm answers. Maybe I could start at the top and work my way down slowly.

"Well, well, well," Wornar drawled.

"One of my favourite sources of water," Ryze drawled. His eyes glinted dangerously. I suspected the only thing keeping him from killing Wornar was wondering why the hells he was here in the first place.

Wornar smirked. "Always with the ridiculous comments. So predictable."

"I won't say the same about you," Ryze said. "What the fuck are you doing here?"

Wornar raised his hand to admire his own fingernails. "One of my contacts told me those lost courts returned. It was a simple matter to realise, sooner or later, they'd come here, wanting their land back. I thought it prudent to come and warn King Mikohal of that possibility. My apologies, that *probability*," he corrected. "I didn't quite anticipate your involvement, but I should have. You can't help but stick your nose in places it doesn't belong."

Vayne gripped my hand and growled. "At least he doesn't stick his cock where it doesn't belong."

Wornar laughed. "Is that what she told you? That she didn't enjoy every moment of fucking me?" He took a step towards me. He locked his eyes on mine and continued.

"She loved every bit of it. She begged me to pound my cock into her pussy. She loved pleasing me. She loved the feeling of my cum between her legs."

My stomach turned and suddenly the feeling of Zared's cum on my thighs didn't feel so exciting.

"You know as well as I do all of that is a lie," I said

coldly. "You violated me. You violated the alpha-omega connection. You used it for your own twisted enjoyment. I hated every single touch."

He stepped closer and I had to force myself not to flinch. He was so close I smelled the alpha scent all over him. Even now, some tiny amount of omega instinct wanted me to please him.

Fortunately, the amount was so tiny I could dismiss it, but not before that made my stomach turn too.

He raised one eyebrow and said, "I don't care. You're one insignificant, worthless, omega slut. Your opinion of me is entirely irrelevant. What matters right now is that you are aligned with the court that would make war on poor, innocent humans."

Only Vayne's hand in mine kept me from blasting him to oblivion. Forget the seven hells, he wouldn't even be in enough pieces to go there.

"What have you done with the King?" Cavan asked.

Wornar's gaze slid off me like a snake. "I have done nothing but warn him of the enemy on his doorstep. I have assured him the Spring Court will come to his assistance if you should try to press the matter."

Tavian started to laugh. "That's the funniest

thing I've heard in a long time. Even funnier than Ryze's daddy jokes." His smile faded to a brutal, calculating fury. "You realise you would stand against the combined forces of the Winter, Summer and Autumn Courts as well as the courts of Shadow and Dreams."

Wornar tilted his head to the side. "You'd go to war for humans? Have you become that bored?"

"You tell us," Ryze said. "You're also here, provoking conflict. Thiron wouldn't have wanted this."

"Thiron was a fool," Wornar said scathingly. "He would have let you walk all over him. Or better yet, he would have bent over and let you fuck his ass."

"You say ass fucking like it's a bad thing," Tavian remarked. He still had the dangerous look on his face. His hands were at his sides, but I doubted anyone was fooled. He'd have a couple of blades in his hand, and then embedded in Wornar before anyone could blink.

"We'd like to speak to King Mikohal ourselves," Cavan said. "Unless you're declaring war right now, step aside and let us pass." His voice was ice cold fury.

For the first time, Wornar looked uncertain, but that didn't last more than half a heartbeat. It was immediately replaced with his usual slick smile.

"Of course, I don't think you'll be welcome. In fact, I should escort you. Humans are known for acting rashly. I wouldn't want any of you to die the moment you step through the door."

The expression on his face said otherwise. His gaze scanned us and settled on Zared. He briefly looked confused, but shook his head and looked away. He must have recognised Zared, but didn't understand how he was now Fae.

I sure as fuck wasn't going to explain it to him.

He turned on his booted heel and gestured for the Fae who accompanied him to proceed us all back into the castle.

"Keep your eyes out for an ambush," Vayne whispered, his mouth next to my ear.

He didn't need to tell me that, all my senses were on alert for anything Wornar might try to pull. I trusted him as far as I could spit him.

Not, I thought, grimacing to myself, that I'd want him anywhere near my mouth.

"Can I just kill him?" Tavian asked Ryze.

"Not yet," Ryze said regretfully.

"What about me?" Zared asked. "Can I kill him?"

"Not you either," Ryze said wearily. "We need to

find out what's really going on here. We can't do that if he's dead."

"Listen to Ryzellius," Wornar said over his shoulder. "You'll never understand the situation if you kill me. Not to mention the fact that the king would definitely not speak to you if you commit an act of aggression in his castle."

"Wouldn't want to leave a puddle of blood on his pretty tiles," Vayne said sarcastically. "Fuck that, yes I would."

Wornar clicked his tongue. "So bloodthirsty. Ryze, it's past time you had your subordinates under control. Perhaps you should surround yourself with more omegas and order them to protect and respect you."

Only my hand on Vayne's stopped him from lunging at Wornar and driving his sword through his chest. I didn't know why I stopped myself. If it wasn't for Ryze telling the others not to kill Wornar, I might not have bothered.

"I don't need to order people to respect and protect me," Ryze said to Wornar. "They do it willingly. It's you they don't respect, because you're a shithead. Does King Mikohal know you're a rapist?"

I thought Wornar might get angry and give us an excuse to kill him, but instead he laughed.

"That's such a harsh word for someone who always takes what he wants too," Wornar said lightly.

"Did you give Khala a choice of which alpha she spent her first heat with? Don't answer that, I know you didn't. The only option you presented her with was yourself. You as good as forced yourself on her. And you didn't even tell her she might be part Fae. No, she had to find that out for herself. I gather it was extremely unpleasant for her. You consider yourself so much better than me, In the end, you and I are very much alike."

I felt Ryze's fury through the bond and his struggle to keep from planting his fist in Wornar's face.

In addition to that, I felt a surge of remorse. As ugly as Wornar's words were, they were also painfully accurate. Ryze did do all those things, but not out of malice or the need to control me. He did it because he didn't want me to get hurt. There was a world of difference between that and what Wornar did to me.

Wornar was wrong, they were nothing alike.

We passed through doors big enough to fit a carriage and a couple of horses, and into the castle itself.

Humans who were occupied with their daily

tasks stopped to stare at us. One woman almost lost hold of a basketful of laundry. She caught it at the last minute before hurrying away.

Several children stopped to stare, eyes wide, mouths opened. I offered them a smile, but none smiled back. They didn't look scared, just overwhelmed.

"The throne room is through here." Wornar led the way as if he thought he owned the place.

The further we went, the more uneasy I felt. It wasn't just being in Wornar's company, it was something more than that. He was definitely up to something, I just didn't know what.

I found myself walking with Cavan on one side of me and Ryze on the other. Tavian and Zared walked ahead and Vayne behind. The message was clear. If anyone touched me, they would be dealt with.

If they managed to get close enough.

We stepped into the throne room. It was sparsely decorated, like the rest of Phikus. Function instead of form.

One wall was lined with narrow windows, wide enough for an archer to fire through. Not big enough for a person to climb in or out.

The other wall was covered in tapestries

depicting past kings and queens. They all seemed to have a fondness for black horses.

The ceiling was lined with beams of dark wood that looked like they'd hung there for hundreds of years. The stone floor was worn smooth from thousands and thousands of passing feet.

A long, woollen carpet led the way from the door to the foot of a throne made of the same heavy wood as the ceiling beams. The throne itself was covered with no carvings, no decorations, no gems inset in the surface. The only remotely ornate aspect of it was a padded cushion on the seat. Even that was relatively simple.

Unlike Fae, it was easier to discern the ages of humans. King Mikohal was in his middle fifties, lines on his face, grey heavily sprinkled through his hair. His brown eyes were bright and clear, He looked weary. And wary.

He seemed as cautious of Wornar as he was of the rest of us. He was dressed in simple leather pants, and a cotton shirt laced at the chest. His feet were covered in boots that reached to just under his knees.

If he wasn't seated on a throne, I would have taken him for a huntsman, or maybe a soldier.

When I was human, I would have found him

attractive. On some level, I still did, but the glance he gave me said it wouldn't be reciprocated because of how I now looked, and the company I kept.

Honestly, I wasn't too impressed with the company he kept, either.

"Your Highness," Wornar said smoothly, with a hint of sarcasm. "As I told you, Fae have come to take your kingdom from you. I told them you wouldn't allow it, but they insisted upon speaking to you. They are most insistent these lands don't belong to you."

Mikohal regarded us with a steady look. He was careful, but not afraid.

"Your Highness." Ryze gave him a bow. "Allow me to introduce myself. I'm High Lord Ryzellius of the Winter Court. Wornar here is mistaken about our intentions." He jerked his thumb towards Wornar.

His lack of title didn't go unnoticed by Wornar, who looked irritated.

Mikohal stood slowly. "Are you suggesting you haven't come on behalf of the Court of Shadows to ask for Fraxius to be returned to them? Or that at the very least, you expect us to reside with them and be subservient to them as we once were?"

"No one said you had to be subservient," Ryze said.

"But you do not deny the rest?" Mikohal asked.

"I cannot deny that we have come on their behalf to ask," Ryze admitted. "But—"

Mikohal nodded at Wornar just as I realised what was off about the atmosphere in the room.

"Kill them," Wornar ordered.

"They're all omegas!" I shouted as a dozen Fae closed in on us.

21

KHALA

I shuddered under the pressure of Wornar's order. I didn't feel the need to obey, but it still weighed down heavily on me.

Was this how Zared and Vayne felt when they were encased in stone? I gritted my teeth and shook it off.

The pack had swords and knives in their hands, or magic ready, but none moved to use them. Not yet. Instead, they arrayed themselves around me, facing outward. All five of them felt confident, but waiting. Biding their time. Not one would make a rash move. If they did, it might cost them their lives. No, they needed clear heads and they knew it.

The Spring Court omegas moved in closer, wary.

Some looked eager to kill us, many didn't. It was the latter which made up my mind.

I thought taking a life might be difficult.

Especially when it wasn't in self-defence. When no one was wielding a sword, about to remove my head from my shoulders. Or had an arrow aimed at my heart.

Wornar wielded no weapon of his own. No knife. No magic as far as I could tell. He stood off to the side, watching, expecting his weapons to do his work for him.

In the end, it was easy to slide magic under his skin. Through his chest and into his heart. It was a simple matter of curling magic around the organ and making it stop.

The widening of his eyes was the only indication that he understood what was happening. An accusing glance in my direction. His whole body froze. He toppled to the ground.

The reluctant omegas froze. Several took hurried steps back, hastily lowering weapons. A couple looked around in confusion, as if they had no idea where they were or how they got there.

The remaining four shook their heads, unde-cided, until one lept at Ryze.

She got a blade through her forehead from

Tavian for her trouble. The other three separated and lunged at Vayne, Cavan and Zared.

Vayne made quick work of his opponent with a couple of parries and slashes with his sword.

Cavan incinerated the third without raising a sweat. A pile of ashes lay on the floor at his feet, still smoldering for a long while.

We all turned to Zared as he parried with his new sword. He never told me where he got that from. It was a much better sword than the one he used to carry. And he was better with it than the last time I saw him use one. Then, Ryze intervened, firing an arrow into the forehead of Zared's opponent.

Now, Zared held his own, pushing the Fae back further and further before he got the chance to run his blade through the man's chest. He gave Ryze a look when the High Lord started to applaud.

"You really do know how to use a sword," Ryze teased, but his expression was approving.

"I can practice on you if you'd like," Zared said dryly.

Ryze grinned in response and crouched down beside Wornar. "That was almost anticlimactic."

He pressed his fingers to Wornar's neck. "He's definitely dead. It seems like he just...dropped down dead. Perhaps his heart gave out under the pressure of his new duties." He clicked his tongue. "I did tell him being High Lord was a lot of work and stress. He should have listened."

He glanced up at me and smiled. He clearly knew what I did, but this way there would be no retribution for assassinating Wornar. It was nothing more than a sad tragedy.

In reality, it was bittersweet. Vengeance didn't feel as good as I thought it would. Whatever I was expecting, it wasn't the hollow feeling inside. Maybe later, the full extent of what I did would sink in.

Either way, Wornar was dead and the omegas acting under his orders were free from him.

Mikohal flopped back down on his throne and shook his head. "What in the name of the gods?"

"Wornar was controlling their minds," Ryze told him. "When he died so suddenly, it broke the connection. They are free to return to the Spring Court."

He gave them a meaningful look. Something along the lines of, 'get the hells out of here before I change my mind.'

They scattered like petals in the breeze, hurrying out the door without looking back.

Mikohal rubbed a hand over his forehead and

eyes. "I didn't realise Fae had such an ability." For the first time, he looked slightly scared.

"We don't," Ryze said. "Only certain Fae and only over other certain Fae. We couldn't do that to you." He didn't elaborate any further.

"You won't force me to surrender my land?" Mikohal asked carefully.

"I can't and I won't," Ryze assured him. "All I want is to work out some compromise that suits everyone. That may prove difficult, if not impossible. The Court of Shadows currently resides in caves. I'm sure you'd agree that's no way to live."

"Neither is constant suspicion of one's neighbours," Mikohal said. "I fear that's what will result from letting them return here. However..." He looked thoughtful, if somewhat reluctant. "There is a place, if they're willing to work at clearing the land and building their homes from scratch."

"What place?" Cavan asked slowly.

"Allow me to show you." Mikohal rose. "If you'll please come this way." He gestured towards the door, indicating that we should follow him out.

He led the way to a small library. All right, a large library, but small compared to the one in the Winter Court.

Along one wall hung a map. It showed all four of

the seasonal courts, their names written in a flowing script. Beside them were the three human lands, Fraxius, Freid and Gerian. The map also showed an island far out to sea. On that island was a small image of a griffin. The only thing missing was Nallis, as far as I could tell.

"Here," Mikohal pointed to a jut of land to the south of Fraxius. "Myself and the King of Gerian have spoken many times as to who owns this land. Both countries claim it as their own. We often have border skirmishes over that land. Most of our wars have been fought over it. Perhaps giving that piece of land to the Court Of Shadows would be a compromise that may satisfy both countries."

"You think the King of Gerian will give up any claim he has over it?" Cavan asked.

"Not easily," Mikohal conceded. "But faced with the possible alternative of handing over land we already occupy to the Fae, then perhaps he will understand it may result in fewer conflicts."

"Or more conflicts," Tavian said softly.

"Potentially," Mikohal agreed. "I won't claim it's an easy compromise. My own people may strenuously object, but I see no clear alternative."

"Neither do I," Ryze said. "Now would be a good time to establish the council Cavan would like us to have. In my experience, open communication is the best way to prevent further misunderstanding."

Cavan raised an eyebrow at him.

Ryze smiled. "It took me a while, but I got there."

Cavan shook his head, but smiled back. "A Council of High Lords, High Ladies and Kings might be the quickest way to reach an agreement."

"And Queens," Mikohal said. "Freid has a queen now." For some reason, he looked amused at that.

I wasn't sure if it was because he thought women shouldn't rule, or if there was more to it.

"Ah, and Queens," Ryze said. "I'm more than happy to host such an auspicious gathering."

Cavan looked like he might object, but he gestured his agreement after a few moments. "I'll send word to Hycanthe, Illaria, Vernissa and whoever will take over from Wornar."

"No assholes," Tavian said.

"No assholes," Cavan agreed. "I gather Wornar has a younger brother who is much less ambitious than he was. With any luck, we can convince the Spring Court to accept him as High Lord."

While they talked amongst themselves, I looked more closely at the map.

"What is it?" Zared placed a hand on my shoulder and leaned in to look too.

"That has to be where the Court of Dreams ended up." I pointed at the island. "It was right here all along and we didn't know."

"It was also right there in the room you slept for ten years," he said. "This might have been another clue for us to find if we came here instead of doing all the things we did. Or it might be a coincidence. Someone went there at some point and saw they were griffins, so they added it to the map. They might have had no clue there were Fae there too."

"You're right," I conceded. "I just wonder what else there is out there we didn't find."

"Like an island full of dragons?" Tavian stepped over to the other side of me and laughed softly. He had that glow about him that he always had after he killed someone.

"Maybe," I said, giving a laugh of my own. "What would you do if there was an island on this map and it had a dragon on it?"

"That's easy, I'd tell Ryze. He'd organise the ship and we'd sail there to take a look. He wouldn't be able to resist the lure of an adventure like that."

"Going to a place that might have dragons would probably not end very fucking well," Vayne said over my shoulder. "With my luck, I'd get eaten. Not in the good way." His lips brushed the side of my neck.

"But you'd go anyway," I said.

"Someone has to keep Ryze and Tavian out of trouble," Vayne replied. "Besides, if they go, you'd go, and wherever you go, I go. So yes, I'd go."

"So would I," Zared said. "Wherever you go, I go. You can't even send me back to Havenmoor any more."

"Are you all right with that?" I asked him gently. "Neither of us can go back there again."

"I don't want to go back," he said steadily. "I want to move forward. With you and our pack."

I smiled and lightly kissed his mouth. "Good, because that's what I want too."

The past was the past and I didn't want to think about it anymore. I made a note to mention to Ryze and Cavan that the council should discuss the Silent Maidens, and what was best for them, now and in the future. They deserved to understand what was happening to them and why. We needed to find a better way to ascertain who was an omega long before they went into heat.

I might even be able to tell who would transition and who wouldn't. That would change a lot of things.

"Although, I wouldn't mind having a bit of peace and quiet after this," I added. "Now the lost courts aren't lost anymore and Wornar is dead, maybe we can relax. I can't remember the last time I sat down and read a good book."

"Neither can I," Tavian said. "I can recommend one about a Fae with wings who goes into this weird human world. It even has a talking cat in it."

Vayne snorted. "How do people think up these things?" He rolled his eyes toward the ceiling.

"It's called having an imagination," Tavian told him. "Maybe you should try it sometime."

"I have a very good imagination." Vayne sniffed. "Right now, I'm imagining Khala naked, her mouth around my cock."

"Funny, I imagine that quite often," Tavian said.

"Me too," Zared said. "I also imagine Tavian's mouth around my cock. I guess that means I'm more imaginative than Vayne."

Vayne shook his head. "No, I could imagine that too, I just don't want to."

"Sure," Tavian drew out the word. "I bet you imagine it all the time, and that's all right. If you imagine it often enough, it might even happen." He wiggled his eyebrows at Vayne, who simply muttered something under his breath in response.

"*W*ornar's brother seems heartbroken at his loss," Ryze said sarcastically.

I snorted softly. "I'd noticed that. It would seem Rian recently discovered Wornar was responsible for Thiron's death. I would assume from that, his days were numbered. His sudden death in such a tragic manner took care of the problem for the Spring Court."

My only regret was not incinerating Wornar myself, but Khala killing him the way she did made things easier for everyone. Except perhaps for her. She seemed conflicted about what she'd done. I understood that.

Taking a life wasn't something anyone should do lightly, no matter what they did to deserve it. I would have been surprised if she enjoyed it as much as Tavian seemed to. She wasn't the bloodthirsty type. She was practical and did what needed to be done.

I glanced over the wide table and watched Rian as he spoke to Illaria. He looked very much like his brother, but without the predatory glint in his eyes.

"I heard a rumour," Ryze started.

I turned to him and grimaced. "I don't think I should listen to any sentence that starts with that. Especially after the last twenty years. Rumours have a way of sometimes being partly true, and sometimes not."

I'd likely always be curious as to why the stories of the two lost courts got so mixed up. I don't suppose it mattered much, but I was naturally curious and liked nothing more than learning and understanding new things.

No, that's not accurate, I loved nothing more than Khala, but learning new things was high on my list.

Ryze grinned. "You'll like this one."

I sighed. "Fine. Are you going to make me ask or are you going to tell me?" Trust him to find yet another way to taunt me. He seemed to have made it his life's work over the last couple of weeks. Naturally, I gave it back, and then some.

I couldn't let someone like him get the better of me. In addition, a little healthy competition never hurt anyone. It kept things interesting between us. Or maybe it was just our way of skirting around whatever might be forming between Ryze and I.

I didn't know what that was yet, and I didn't think he did either. I doubted we'd ever have the kind of relationship with each other that we had with Khala, or that Tavian and Zared had, but he was slightly more tolerable than I'd spent the last couple of hundred years thinking he was.

I might not admit it to myself, but he could kiss.

"I think I should make you ask." The asshole smiled more broadly.

I shook my head. "You're such a prick."

He laughed. "So I've been told." He picked up a piece of cheese from the platter in front of him and popped it into his mouth. "I heard a rumour that Rian and at least two other Fae men are in a relationship with a human woman. Apparently, she lives in the Spring Court with them."

My eyebrows rose. "That is interesting. Most human women would run from an arrangement like that. She must be very impressive." After I lost Alivia to Terald, I was bitter towards humans for a long time.

Now I'd come to realise the only important thing in life was love. I thought about taking Khala back home to see her parents, but I suspected she wasn't ready for that yet. Some day she would be. And if she wasn't, I wouldn't press the issue. That was her choice to make.

"Any woman who would put up with one man, much less several, might be considered impressive," Ryze said. "Some of us can be a pain in the ass at times." He quirked an eyebrow at me.

"I see you're referring to yourself," I said dryly. I watched vaguely as Khala and Zared led the two human kings and the human queen into the conference room. They looked anxious to be surrounded by so many Fae, but they took their seats with their backs straight, chins raised.

I hoped this meeting would dispel some myths about Fae for them. And vice versa. It was past time for some serious change and today was the start of that.

"Not one asshole present," Ryze observed. "Apparently Illaria quietly... 'took care' of Harel. No more Wornar. Even you and I get along."

"Will wonders never cease?" I asked.

"Hopefully not," he said. "Life would be boring without any wonders in it."

"The gods forbid you'd get bored," I said drolly. "I can only imagine the things you'd get up to to keep yourself amused."

"You're starting to sound like Vayne." Ryze took a sip of water from his clay cup.

"I didn't realise Vayne was so wise." I took a sip of my own water. I would have preferred wine, but we agreed we should start the meeting with clear heads. Wine would have to wait until later.

"Of course he is. He wouldn't be the commander of my army if he wasn't wise." He eyed me like I planned to poach Vayne after all.

I thought about it, but the pack spent so much time between the Winter Court and the Summer Court that I saw Vayne almost daily. Having him work for me would be potentially awkward. Better to leave that to Ryze.

Khala stepped around the table and leaned down between us. Gods, she always smelled so good. Even better now she was close to her heat again. So was Tavian. I fully intended to make sure I was present for both of them. If they went together...all the better.

"Everyone's here," she said. "Will you start the meeting?"

Although the meeting was taking place in the Winter Court, they all agreed I should speak first.

"This was your idea," Tavian had pointed out. "You've been trying to unite us all for twenty years. It seems appropriate to me." He shrugged.

No one argued with him, not even Ryze.

"THAT WENT WELL, for the most part." I took a long sip of wine.

As we had anticipated, the King of Gerian wasn't impressed with the proposal to give land to the Court of Shadows.

He was even less impressed at the suggestion he could give up the part of the country he actually *could* claim. Of course, he argued that Fae should live on Fae land. We'd gone around and around on the subject for a couple of hours before coming to a tentative agreement.

The Court of Shadows would occupy the land for the time being and we would see how things went.

Meanwhile, the Court of Dreams would return to the island and make their life there. From what Hycanthe said, none of the griffin riders objected to that arrangement. All they wanted to do was live their lives with their beasts and not put them at risk again. Since no one wanted the giant creatures in their cities, no one argued that decision. Hycanthe's well practised glare helped in that regard.

To my surprise, the humans actually asked about running hot water. The easiest part of the meeting was offering to show them how to install and use it. That had helped sway the King of Gerian to our way of thinking about that contested piece of land. That was understandable; a hot bath was a lot better than conflict any day.

We were almost finished, when Khala asked to address Vernissa.

"Since you have land out in the sun, I'd like to suggest you discontinue the practice of culling older Fae."

The room fell silent in shock, before people started to mutter. The humans in particular. They seemed very surprised Fae would undertake such a barbaric practice.

"If we no longer have to limit our numbers, then we can certainly reconsider the practice," Vernissa replied, not meeting anyone's eye.

"I don't see any reason why you have to limit

yourselves," Khala told her. She looked around the table. "Does anyone?"

Most of us shook our heads, but the King of Gerian looked like he might disagree.

"If your numbers grow, you may need more land," he said finally.

"It would take several generations for that possibility," I told him. "Fae generations. Hundreds of years. I promise you, it will be no concern of yours or many many of your descendants."

Eventually it might be a problem, but not in the near enough future to matter to any of us. That would be an issue when and if it became one.

He seemed mollified at that. "Then I don't suppose it matters what I think. I would prefer the murder of people just because they're older to not catch on." His tone was gruff, but his bearded face curled up in a smile. Given he was at least in his late sixties, that was a sensible standpoint.

Vernissa was visibly unimpressed at hearing it referred to that way, but she got the biggest concession for her and her court. They would live their lives in the sun, like they wanted to.

I wondered if any of them would stay underground, in spite of saying they'd follow her wherever she led. That was a matter for them.

"In the end, that was much more civilised than when we met up at Nallis," Ryze said. "Although, in the past, it was more likely someone would turn up with an army, not for a friendly conversation."

"Are you referring to yourself again?" I asked. I couldn't resist needling him. That was something I didn't think we'd ever stop doing to each other. It was certainly a lot better than trading insults with actual bad intentions behind them.

"Probably." He grinned. He swirled his whiskey around in his glass and took a sip. "We've all come a long way since then."

"Especially you two," Tavian remarked. He sat on the couch beside Khala, her feet in his lap. "Which I have to admit I'm conflicted about." He pulled off her socks and started to rub her feet.

We all turned to him and waited for him to elaborate.

"On one hand, seeing you kiss was one of the hottest things I've ever seen in my life. On the other hand, if you two get along with each other, we won't have to sneak into the Summer Court ever again."

He sighed exaggeratedly. "I enjoyed doing that. I've been thinking, I might take on a few jobs as an assassin again. I miss sneaking and killing."

"Whatever makes you happy," Ryze told him.

"As long as you don't assassinate me," Vayne said with a grunt.

"I'll only assassinate you if someone pays me a lot of money to do it," Tavian said. He smiled lopsidedly.

Khala socked him on the arm. "No assassinating Vayne," she scolded. "No matter how much money someone offers you to do it."

Tavian pouted playfully. "Fine, just for you, I promise not to assassinate Vayne."

She gave him a steady look.

"Or anyone else in the pack," he added. "The only thing I'll stick inside any of them is my cock."

She nodded, satisfied. "That goes for all of you. No killing each other."

"You're a hard woman," Ryze joked. "What if we want you to kill us so you can bring us back to life? I've always been curious about what that would be like."

She and Tavian exchanged a look and started laughing.

He raised his hand in question, but shook his head when he got no answer from them. "Young Fae these days." He smiled indulgently.

"Finally," Vayne said. "Ryze admits he's old."

Ryze stuck his middle finger up at him. "I am not fucking old, they're just young.

From the chair in the corner, Zared groaned. "I just realised I have hundreds of years to spend with all of you."

"Fuck, me too," Vayne said.

That only made Tavian and Khala laugh harder.

I couldn't help smiling at all of them.

23

KHALA

I trailed my fingers across the surface of the conference table. If I wasn't there myself, I might not believe so many important people sat around it only hours earlier.

Honestly, I was surprised they all turned up. The three human leaders in particular. They were all both willing and curious. More open-minded than Harel had been. More receptive to change than I think any of us expected.

When I thought back to how scared I used to be of the Fae, I felt somewhat silly. What I was afraid of, was the unknown. Now I knew Fae in general weren't scary, any more than humans were. There were bad Fae, just as they were bad humans, but bylarge most were reasonably harmless.

And those who weren't, fate caught up with them sooner or later.

"This is where you got to," Ryze said softly. He stepped into the room, followed by Cavan. "We were starting to worry."

"I wasn't worried," Cavan said. "But I was curious. You seemed...contemplative."

"Yes, that's exactly it," Ryze agreed. "It was a lot of deep thought for this place." He smiled.

"I'm sure deep thought happens a lot here." I let him wrap his large hands around my hips and lift me until I was sitting on the conference table, between his legs.

"A lot of deep something," he agreed. He leaned in and kissed me lightly.

Cavan regarded us both for a moment or two. He stepped back over to the door.

I thought he was about to leave, but instead he turned the lock until it clicked into place.

That small act made my blood heat and race through my veins. I'd been with all of the guys in different combinations, but never just the two High Lords. The idea made me hot and wet between the thighs.

All right, when was I not hot and wet between my thighs these days?

Ryze eased me down so I lay on my back in front of them both. He ran his hands up and down my body before undoing the front of my pants and sliding them down my hips.

Cavan stepped around to the side of the table and undid the buttons of my shirt, one by one. He peeled the sides away, exposing my breasts.

"I have never seen anyone more beautiful," he said softly. He leaned down to press feather light kisses on my nipples.

"Thank you," Ryze said, as though Cavan was speaking to him. He pulled the gusset of my panties aside and kissed the inside of my thigh and up to my pussy.

Cavan snorted softly without stopping as he delivered a circle of tiny kisses around my breast. Every so often, he'd graze the tip of his nose, or his cheek, against my nipple. The slightest touch sent white hot heat through me, making me shiver with anticipation.

Ryze teased all around my clit and entrance, barely touching, taunting.

"Please," I said breathlessly.

"Please, what?" Ryze asked.

"Please, sir." They were going to drive me wild

with their gentle touches and brushes. "Sirs," I corrected.

"I think she's asking to be our dirty little slut." Cavan kissed the underside of my breast.

Ryze's eyebrows rose in a combination of surprise and curiosity. "Is that right?" He cocked his head at me. "Are you begging to be our dirty slut?"

"Yes, sir," I replied. I swallowed hard. "I'm yours to fuck." If they didn't soon, I was going to go out of my mind. My hand drifted down to my pussy and over my clit, before Ryze gripped my wrists and pressed both of them against the tabletop above my head.

"That's our job," he scolded lightly. "We're the ones who are going to make you come, not yourself. Right, Cav?"

"Correct," Cavan agreed. "We'll make her scream."

"I like the sound of that." Ryze leaned down further and ran his tongue from my rear hole, all the way up to my clit. "Mmmm, delicious. Hands down the tastiest meal ever to be eaten at this table."

I moaned at the jolt of lightning that shot all the way through me, from my toes, to the top of my head. He'd barely touched me, but I knew what he'd feel when he slipped the tip of his finger inside my pussy.

"She's so wet. I think you're right about her wanting to be our slut." He slid his finger in and out of me a few times before adding a second one.

"I don't think she's ever been so wet in her life. I could make several portals just out of her pussy." He was clearly impressed.

"Of course she is, because she's a good girl," Cavan said. "She's the best girl."

I couldn't decide what I liked better, being called a good girl, or the dirty talk. In the end, I decided I liked all of it.

Especially when Ryze said, "She's a good little slut."

He licked me again, more firmly this time, while gently but smoothly fucking me with his fingers.

Cavan fastened his mouth around my nipple and began to suck, just as gentle and teasing as Ryze. After a minute or two, he switched to the other nipple, tasting me lightly with his tongue before drawing my tender flesh between his lips and sucking more firmly.

Through the bond, I saw myself how they saw me. They loved the way I moaned and writhed, and shivered at their touch. I saw their excitement at driving me closer and closer to the edge. I felt it build as their touch became firmer. All of their attention was on me and wanting me to come.

I pressed my palms against the cool top of the conference table as I shattered into too many pieces to count. Probably something beyond infinity. I was overwhelmed with the feeling of bliss and their arousal at my sounds and movement. So overwhelmed, I plunged over the edge into an even deeper abyss. One I would have happily stayed in with them forever.

Ryze lifted his shining face and carefully swivelled me around to face Cavan as the other High Lord unfastened the front of his pants and freed his erection.

Cavan gripped my hips and pulled me onto his cock. With almost painful slowness, he impaled me all the way to his knot.

He waited for me to get used to him, before pushing inside a little further. Bit by bit, my muscles stretched to take in his knot.

I didn't think it was possible, until he was fully seated inside me. I was stretched almost all the way to the limit, and it felt utterly incredible. He was touching me everywhere inside and out in exactly the right place and precisely the right way.

"Gods," I breathed. "That feels incredible."

"You feel incredible," he said. He ran his hands up and down my sides, his hips still until finally he started to move slowly. He slid all the way out of me, before impaling me to his knot again.

Ryze pushed his own pants down to the top of his thighs and gripped my chin between his thumb and forefinger. He turned my face towards him and pressed his cock against my lips. "Open up, there's a good slut."

I smiled at him with my eyes and opened my mouth to take in his thick length almost to the back of my throat. His cock was so warm and hard, yet smooth against my lips. I'd always enjoyed sucking cocks, but these five guys had the best that ever passed my lips. So firm, throbbing and giving. Everything a girl could want in a cock.

I kept my gaze on Ryze while he rolled his hips, sliding himself in and out of my mouth.

"So fucking good," he said breathlessly.

"So very good," Cavan agreed. He thrust faster, then slower, then faster again, always careful with his knot. He wanted to wreck my pussy, not break her.

They found a rhythm and started to build towards their own orgasms.

I let them feel how they felt, moving in and out

of my body with even, deliberate strokes. I showed them how good it was to have two, incredible men fucking me at the same time. And how much I loved both of them.

I felt love back from them, in a wave of devoted adoration. I'd never felt as loved in my life as I did then. That increased by three, when the other men sent their own warmth and love down the bond.

Along with some envy on the part of Vayne that it wasn't his cock down my throat. I told him he could get a turn later. That seemed to mollify him.

Between all of that and the way Cavan's knot brushed over my clit with each thrust, I tumbled over the edge for a third time.

I arched my back and screamed toward the ceiling, the sound muffled by Ryze's cock and his cum as he spilled himself into my mouth. I swallowed down every drop quickly, before I choked on the delicious mouthful.

Cavan came at the same time, stilling and grunting as his hot cum rushed out of his tip and into my body.

As one, we all sagged, panting and waiting for our blood to cool.

"That was even better than deep thought," Ryze said.

I slipped my mouth off his cock and laughed softly. "There's a time and place for everything."

"It's always a good time and place for showing you how we feel about you," he said. He pulled his pants up and leaned over to kiss my mouth. "I love you."

"I love you too," I told him. "If you're not careful, I'll get used to all this love."

"We'll make sure you get used to it." Cavan eased his cock out of me and did up his own pants. "Because none of us is going anywhere without you."

"You better not," I said in a mock growl. "I might decide not to be a good girl after all."

"If you aren't a good girl, then I'm going to have to spank your ass," Cavan said in a mock growl of his own.

I grinned. "In that case, I'm going to be very, very bad."

*W*ind whipped hair across my face. I brushed it off and stepped over closer to the rubble. What was once a proud castle, was now nothing more than a pile of stones, splintered wood and shards of glass. Anyone who moved around here, had to tread carefully to keep from stepping on anything sharp or dangerous.

"We were fucking lucky we got out in time," Vayne remarked. He stood with his arms crossed, taking in the sight with an unusually sombre expression. Even for him. We'd come close to dying, but we hadn't. We were two of the lucky ones. Two of all too few.

"Did they find Dennin and Ramela?" He tore his

eyes away from the ruins long enough to glance at Hycanthe.

"It took five days of searching, but they did." It was Jezalyn who answered. "They seemed very determined to find them."

"They wanted to know for sure they were dead," Hycanthe said flatly.

She'd gone into heat two days ago. As a result, she seemed more relaxed than she had before. She appeared very much like she found her place in the world. A challenging one, to be sure, but something she could be a part of and be proud of.

I was happy for her. For both of them. As happy as anyone could be while standing amongst a place that held the memory of so much death.

I remembered the children who ran around kicking the ball. Some of them got out in time, but many didn't. It was always the innocent who got caught up in situations made by others for reasons that had nothing to do with them. The fact it was children, compounded the heartbreak for all of us.

"They actually found six people still alive." Jezalyn smiled, clearly thinking back on the last few days. "Five of them children. A couple were badly injured, but Hycanthe healed them. She's become like a hero to the court." She turned fond eyes on her lover.

"Jezalyn might be exaggerating slightly," Hycanthe said. "I did what I had to do, that was all." A blush crept up her cheeks.

"And they love you for it," Jezalyn told her. "Almost as much as I do." She kissed Hycanthe's cheek.

"There's nothing wrong with owning what you can do," I said. I sent a quick thanks to any of the gods who might be listening for sparing those five young lives. They were lucky to have not only made it through the collapse of the castle, but to have her there to heal their bodies. No doubt it would take longer to heal their minds.

"You're going to rebuild the castle?"

"Down off the hill." Hycanthe seemed pleased with the change of subject. "The griffins are good at picking up the blocks of stone and moving them. They're carrying them down there one by one for the builders. There was talk about leaving the ruins as they are, but everyone agreed they didn't want a reminder of the past. They're looking to the future. The new Court Of Dreams is going to be built on a brand-new foundation. We're all excited about what we're making here."

"We really are," Jezalyn agreed. "We're a community." Her eyes shone with pride and unshed tears. "Everyone has been amazing and willing to pitch in whenever they're needed. We have griffin riders cooking and doing laundry, and farmers helping to take care of the griffins. For a while there, I was worried they wouldn't accept us. None of them knew us. Why should they follow people they don't know? But everyone has been wonderful. All anyone wants is a fresh start. And to be able to travel to Jorius, and go into heat as the gods intended."

Hycanthe rubbed a hand over the back of her neck. "We need some more alphas, if the other courts can spare them. At the moment, we have only two, and four omegas. And I'm not sharing Jezalyn with anyone." She glanced at me and Tavian as though either of us might possibly try to poach her lover.

I resisted the urge to roll my eyes and nodded instead. "I'll put the word out. I'm sure there are plenty of alphas and omegas who'd welcome the chance to be part of a court that's building itself the way you're doing here. One of the things Cavan wanted was to encourage Fae and humans to move between any courts and countries without sneaking around." Many Fae didn't stay put in the court they were born in, but most did. He wanted them to go where they fit in and were content. That may be a more challenging dream to achieve than it sounded, but we could encourage people. Whatever came from that would come.

I suspected it might cause some tension with Vernissa, if her people decided to leave, but if any court needed fresh blood, it was hers. No doubt she'd welcome new arrivals if that was a choice some wanted to make.

"I think a lot of Fae would love the chance to ride a griffin," I added. No one could deny they were magnificent beasts. I'd never seen anything like them in my life, not even in books.

Vayne grunted. "Only if they're out of their minds."

"I want to ride a griffin," Tavian said from where he crouched beside the rubble.

"I rest my case," Vayne said. He dusted his hands on each other as though wiping the matter away.

Tavian grinned and rose to his feet. "Scared?"

"Yes," Vayne replied. "Yes, I fucking am. It's a long way down off the back of one of those beasts. But if you want to get on one, be my guest." He waved towards a pair who approached, wings outstretched until they landed beside the ruined castle.

They fastened their massive talons around blocks and heaved them up. With what looked like little strain at all, they lifted them several metres off the ground and flew away slowly with them held carefully in front of them.

"They are very useful." Ryze shielded his eyes from the sun with his hand. "I wonder how hard it would be to convince a couple of them to move to the Winter Court."

"What for?" Zared asked.

Ryze considered the question for a moment, but shrugged. "I'm sure I'd think of something."

"I think you want a couple of griffins for the sake of having a couple of griffins," Vayne said. He scowled at Ryze.

"What would be wrong with that?" Ryze asked.

"Griffins eat a lot," Cavan said. "I doubt the Winter Court would want to feed them if they're not productive."

Ryze shrugged. "I'll think of something."

I shook my head at him but smiled. Sometimes the High Lord was more like a young child than a man a few hundred years old. Always looking out for something new and exciting to do or see. So far, I'd managed to talk him out of dying, just so he knew how it felt to be brought back to life. The gods only knew how long that would last. His insatiable curiosity had no bounds.

I wouldn't have him any other way.

A couple more griffins flew in. One went to work picking up a block. The other landed near us.

Vayne took a couple of steps back from the beast, as though concerned she might eat him.

I admit to being slightly nervous in their presence myself. After the attacks, and the battle, they didn't exactly evoke the *best* memories. That was one of the reasons I was here. Partly to check on Hycanthe and Jezalyn to see if they needed any help, and partly to face my fearfulness of the beasts.

I was done living my life in fear. I wanted to face this one head on. The sooner I did that, the sooner I could put it behind me.

"Gavil wanted to talk to you when you came in to check on our progress," Jezalyn told me.

Hycanthe gave him the side eye, but Jezalyn squeezed her hand reassuringly.

I doubted Hycanthe had anything to worry about when it came to any other omega. Jezalyn was a one woman alpha.

I smiled at Gavil as he approached and slipped his helmet off.

"You're looking well," I told him. He looked

slightly less anxious than the last time I saw him. Although, he still wore the misplaced guilt of taking part in the attack on his face.

"I'm feeling well," he replied. "I wanted to thank you for everything you did. Since you came here... everything has changed. Everything is better. Without Patric, Ramela and Dennin we are free. High Lady Hycanthe has already done so much for us. The Court of Dreams may yet live up to its name." He dashed a tear off his cheek.

I might have blinked back a few of my own. It was difficult not to be choked with emotion when I realised what impact I and my pack had on people like him. People who had terrible things done to them, none of which they deserved. He should have spent his life unscarred, going into heat when his body was ready.

Why no one founded an order of Silent Boys, I had no idea. Tavian was lucky to have avoided enduring either.

In the corner of my eye, I caught Jezalyn giving Hycanthe a look that clearly conveyed both pride and a healthy dose of, 'I told you so.'

Hycanthe shrugged and smiled slightly. "I'm just doing what any reasonable person would do."

"Because you're not an asshole," Tavian told her. "That part makes all the difference. Right, Ryze?"

"Right," Ryze replied. "It does, and that in turn helps us to make a real difference. I haven't had to kill anyone from the Summer Court in quite some time. It's remarkably refreshing."

"I hope it's something you'll continue to refrain from doing," Cavan said dryly. "I prefer my people not dead."

"Unless they deserve it," Hycanthe said. She raised her eyebrows at him.

Zared and I may have forgiven and forgotten, but she clearly hadn't. She didn't make trouble over it either though. She had enough on her proverbial plate without picking a fight with Cavan every chance she got.

"Part of our rebuild is going to be a place for Silent Maidens," Hycanthe said. "The omegas here know how it feels to be suppressed. We believe they're best equipped to help those omegas and alphas to deal with their first heat and the choice to suppress themselves if they prefer. Not all omegas want to go through heat. We intend to find a way to do that without suppressing everyone or their ability to speak. It may take some time, but we have plenty of that."

That was an admirable idea. She was right, this was the perfect place for it. I wondered what my life would have been like with a sanctuary like this. Certainly very different to the way it actually went.

"If you need any help, you only have to ask. I'll do whatever I can." I turned back to Gavil and spontaneously gave him a hug. "You're more than welcome. I wish I could have done something sooner, but..."

"The time wasn't right," Cavan said. "You needed to become who you are before you could help everyone else. And you did. All three of you former Silent Maidens did. You've done so much to change...basically the whole world as I know it. Personally, I couldn't be more pleased."

I let him pull me into his arms and kiss me, not caring if we had an audience. Let them watch, it didn't bother me one little bit.

"There's one more matter," Ryze said when we came up for air. "If you'll excuse Khala and I for a few minutes." He offered his hand.

I took it and we walked side by side down the hill. Neither of us said anything until we reached the place where the castle was being rebuilt. Right now, it was nothing more than a patch of cleared land with a pile of blocks beside it. It would take months to build, but no doubt it would be impressive when it was finished.

"Cavan is right," Ryze said finally. "Since meeting you, everything has changed. Well, almost everything. Vayne is still grumpy as fuck. And Tavian still likes killing people for fun. And I still..."

He shook his head. "Some things are the same but most things have changed and they're wonderful. The last few months have been an adventure like nothing else I've ever experienced before. The best thing I ever did in my life was help you get away from that caravan in the rain. You and Zared."

He turned to me and cupped my cheek with his hands. "I love you."

"I love you too," I said softly. "Going with you three that day was the best choice I ever made. At the time, I had no doubt it was the right thing to do, even when I had no idea why or who any of you were. Hells, I didn't even know who *I* was. I don't know if the gods put you in my path, or if it was part of the Court of Dreams' plan. Whatever it was, I'm glad it happened."

He kissed me then, softly at first and then with increasing heat. His hands slid up the back of my shirt and skated over my skin.

"I'll never get enough of you," he said between

kisses. "You and the rest of our pack. You're everything."

I couldn't argue with that. Not just because my mouth was busy, but because he was right. Our pack *was* everything.

I hesitated, mid-kiss as a surge came down the bond. Immediately, my whole body was throbbing and I was wet between my thighs.

"I know I'm a good kisser, but that's not what this is, is it?" Ryze asked.

I shook my head. "No. Tavian is going into heat."

*R*yze threw open a portal to the hill beside the ruin. We leapt through just as Cavan opened one to the Winter Court.

We gathered around Tavian, who was already drenched in sweat, his eyes wide. He was pressed hard against Zared. When he saw Ryze, he grabbed his jacket, dragged him forward and kissed him.

"Let's get back home before this gets messy." Vayne all but shoved us into the portal and out the other side.

The moment Cavan closed the portal behind us, Tavian grabbed him and kissed him.

"I need all of you," he said, his voice hoarse.

"Whatever the omega wants." Ryze manoeuvred all of us towards Tavian's room.

By the time we got there, Tavian was already naked and all but purring between Cavan, Ryze and Zared.

I hesitated at the doorway. Tavian took part in my heat, but he may not want me here at his. It was his choice. He may choose to keep the alphas, or at least one of them, to himself the way Hycanthe would.

I'd understand if that was what he wanted, what he needed. He was the important one right now. Before I could step away, he grabbed my hand and pulled me down on the nest with the rest of them.

"I need you too," he said breathlessly. "Please stay." He pleaded with me with his eyes.

"Of course I'll stay," I said. "I wouldn't want to be anywhere else." Especially with my whole body responding to him the way it was. I was close to my own heat, but not close enough for him to set me off. Not this time anyway.

"Do we need—" Zared gestured over to the table to the side of the room where a half-full bottle of lubricating oil sat.

"No, during heat he makes his own," Ryze said. He was busy shedding his clothes and carelessly tossing them aside.

Vayne tugged me down to the end of the bed and started helping me out of mine.

Zared watched us for a moment with uncertainty, before he stepped over. He grabbed my foot and pulled my pants over it before dropping them on the floor.

Both of them grabbed the side of my panties and tore them right down the middle. Once I was naked, I returned the favour, helping them pull off shirts and slide off pants, and leaving them discarded where they fell. In moments, the floor was covered in a pile of leather, cotton and wool.

I found myself surrounded by five extremely attractive men with very erect cocks.

Fortunately, Tavian's nest was more than big enough to accommodate Ryze and Cavan lavishing attention on him, while I lay between Vayne and Zared. One omega and his alphas and another omega with her two betas. There was more than enough love and cocks to go around.

Tavian was already on all fours, Ryze kneeling beside him. The heat must have made Tavian ready quickly, because Ryze slid his cock straight inside him. He reached around to grip Tavian's cock in firm fingers.

Cavan stroked himself while he watched them fuck.

"You like how that looks?" Zared asked me. "Up on all fours then."

I scrambled up and looked over my shoulder at Zared, who slid his hands up and down my thighs and up to my pussy. He ghosted his fingers over my flesh so lightly I thought I might go crazy. Between that and the heat coursing through the bond, I might come with the slightest touch.

Vayne reached under me to run his hands over my breasts and pinch my nipples. He did that for a while before kneeling beside me and pressing his cock between my lips.

Just as he did that, Tavian came for the first time, and the second, squirting hot cum over Ryze's fingers.

Ryze came a moment later, once, twice. Panting, he moved aside to make room for Cavan. He leaned against one of the posts as the other alpha slipped into Tavian's ass.

Zared started to work me more firmly, fingers sliding in and out. "I think we need that oil after all," he said to Vayne.

Vayne nodded and slipped his cock out of my mouth to get it.

He handed it to Zared who opened it, dipped his fingers inside and worked them into my ass. Stretching me and making me ready with his warm, slippery fingers.

"Please," I pleaded. I needed to feel more inside me. Much more.

Zared slapped my ass once, twice, then slid his hand out of me and positioned his cock there instead. He gripped my hips and slipped his cock inside. He thrust into my ass a few times, then said something to Vayne.

I couldn't make out what it was past the pounding of blood through my ears. It didn't matter. All that mattered was how good he felt inside my body.

Vayne lay down on his back. He looked up at me and smiled. Actually smiled. His expression made my heart flip upside down and inside out. He should smile more often. But if he didn't, that would be all right too. It would make each smile that much more special.

Zared positioned me carefully before he lowered me onto Vayne's cock. He leaned me forward and pressed back into me.

I shivered with the deliciousness of being filled

by both of them. I wanted to close my eyes and savour it, but I couldn't tear my gaze away from Cavan who was pumping heavily into Tavian.

Between the sight, the bond and the heat radiating off the other omega, I was absolutely gone. All I wanted was to get lost in this moment forever.

We all moved in rhythm to Cavan thrusts. All of our eyes on him and Tavian.

When Tavian came again, so did I. And again. And again.

My back arched. I drove myself harder onto Vayne's cock. I was so aroused I might almost have been on heat myself.

I cried out as I drenched Vayne's cock.

"Fuck yeah," Vayne muttered. "Gods, you will never *not* feel good."

"I'm going to come again," I panted. "Come with me. Both of you. All of you."

Tavian gripped Ryze's cock in his hand and worked at him while he rocked back onto Cavan.

"You heard her," he said breathlessly. "We can do this."

We thrust and rocked in near perfect unison before tipping over the edge into a shared oblivion.

We all cried out and panted as the bond was

filled with a sensation of complete and utter bliss. The world could have ended then and there and none of us would have known or cared.

Luckily, it didn't end, but eventually I came down from my rush and lay tangled and panting with Vayne and Zared. For the longest time, we lay and watched Ryze and Cavan swap back and forth, making Tavian feel unbelievably good over and over again.

Eventually, Tavian grew exhausted. He came one more time before flopping down, taking Cavan with him.

"Oh my gods," he panted. "Best heat ever. I thought one alpha was amazing, but two..."

He sighed heavily. "I think I've died and gone somewhere incredible. Definitely no kind of hell. I need a bath, but I want to lie here for a while first."

He smelled of sex and cum, and satisfaction.

He snuggled up in the middle of all of us and nestled down.

"I love all of you," he said sleepily.

"We love you too," I told him.

"We all love you as well." Zared brushed hair off my sweaty face.

"I'm the luckiest Fae woman in the entire world," I whispered. The most loved, the most blessed.

The happiest.

THANK you so much for reading. If you'd love a steamy bonus scene, you cab grab yours here.

My next book is Heartless, Brutal Academy book 1

ABOUT THE AUTHOR

Maggie Alabaster writes reverse harem and, paranormal, sci-fi and fantasy romance.

She lives in NSW, Australia with one spouse, two daughters, one dog, and countless birds.

Sign up for Maggie's newsletter! Sign Up!

Join Maggie's reader group! Join here!

Follow Maggie on Bookbub! Click here to follow me!

Check out Maggie's website- www. maggiealabaster.com

ALSO BY MAGGIE ALABASTER

Brutal Academy

Book 1 Heartless

Book 2 Cruel

Book 3 Vengeful

Court of Blood and Binding

Book 1 Song of Scent and Magic

Book 2 Crown of Mist and Heat

Book 3 Sword of Balm and Shadow

Book 4 Whisper of Frost and Flame

Dark Masque

Book 1 Bait

Book 2 Prey

Book 3 Trap

Saving Abbie

Book 1 Pitch

Book 2 Pound

My Alien Mates

Book 1 Star Warriors

Book 2 Star Defenders

Book 3 Star Protectors

Academy of Modern Magic

Book 1 Digital Magic

Book 2 Virtual Magic

Book 3 Logical Magic

Complete Collection

Summer's Harem

Book 1: Shimmer

Book 2: Glimmer

Book 3: Flicker

Complete collection

Short reads

Taken by the Snowmen

Jingle All the Way

Also by Maggie Alabaster and Erin Yoshikawa

Caught by the Tide

Book 1–Pursued by Shadows

Book 2 Pursued by Darkness

Book 3 Pursued by Monsters